The Green Man.

The Witch Doctor Cases

by

A. D.
Fitzgerald

For the witches, doctors and witch doctors who do their bit to make the world a better place.

With thanks to EJS for the pun which planted the seed.

From the personal papers of B. M.

The thing I hate most about being a Witch is that you lose the simple love of fairy tales.

I still appreciate them, but there is just too much thinly veiled propaganda for me to truly enjoy them any more. The story is always more complicated than what you see on the surface and witches can never take things at face value.

So I have had to forget Hansel and Gretel. The versions people know only tell one side of the story, and that is never enough to get to the truth. The majority of the stories people are now familiar with tend to have the more gruesome details edited out as well, which makes them even less reliable. Those times were brutal, they cherry picked the worst situations and they never let the other side of the story come out. Cultural Propaganda. For each of those witches that got up to no good with curses and traps, there were always others who did what they had to do to help people.

The role of the Witch in the community was a valuable one, if more often misunderstood than appreciated. There were genuinely those times when magic was needed. It was never popular, but sometimes necessary, the same can be said about the practitioners. Whether it was as a healer or advisor the 'good' practitioners of witchcraft were varied in what they did, but there was one unifying feature – they helped people. The real job of the witch was to be there when people ventured from the straight and narrow path of the 'normal' world. This happens quite often as straight and narrow paths are quite frequently at odds with the practicalities of life.

As I said those were the 'good' ones, the less said about those who were more inclined to push people off the path the better. Psychology is often complicated enough, but when you factor in the temptations of power, some people are just incapable of resisting the urge to think their way is better, no matter what the consequences. That is always the personal struggle each witch has to face. Not to give into the temptations. As with a bit of reasoning you might be able to convince yourself that it isn't that dangerous. Not just this once.

This may all sound very good as a theory. That I am just another of those people who think that it is 'cool' to call myself a Witch in the modern world. I have nothing against anyone who wants to call themselves a Witch. To keep the old ways, or the new old ways, burn candles, learn the properties of stones and herbs, try and do a bit of good with their lives and make something of themselves. Make themselves useful. That is all as it should be, and good for them.

The tricky point of terminology then comes. As while they are indeed Witches, they may not be Witches in the same way I am a Witch. The two things are not mutually exclusive, nor are they inextricably entwined. You may encounter a Witch of my type who wouldn't know a bind rune from an astrological symbol. And the other sort who talk about the power of the seasons but can't raise even the faint glimmer of power to even a feather with just their mind.

One isn't better than the other, we are just experiencing different ways to be Witches. It all comes down to an innate ability. The control of what people call 'magic'. Some of the Witches of my type give their skills other names if they find calling it magic distasteful, but they all have the ability to change the world. The 'good' ones work towards keeping people safe from the less normal elements of reality.

What sets us apart is something my old teacher used to call "The knowing". This is not knowledge that anyone who can read books can acquire. It is an instinct that comes from how we interact with the world. For those with the "knowing" the world is much more malleable. I have discussed some of the more extreme theories of quantum physics that look at the underpinning of how the universe works until my head span, but some of it makes sense to me on a level that my academic brain can't quite grasp.

The world is not about what we see on the surface. For those who can look beneath the dimensions that our carefully evolved physical senses use to limit the world, there is a lot more going on. Sometimes the ability lurks hidden in someone for years, sometimes they embrace it at childhood, others feel it but reject it as they fear what they can't frame comfortably into how they have been told the world works – be that by science or religion. People need to find their own way to understanding themselves and only then can they make use of their "knowledge".

Sometimes the desire for change can come before the understanding and that is when the old adage 'be careful what you wish for' is doubly true.

Those who can make their own wishes come to pass have to be more cautious. When there is a conflict between conscious choice and subconscious desire powered by magic that is when things get very dangerous indeed.

And even once we have managed to understand ourselves and find a way to control our desires if we want to use our special powers, we still need to overcome what is possibly the biggest problem for the modern day witch. No one believes in magic anymore. So unless it gets completely out of hand we now have to help in less direct ways.

This means on the whole the modern Witches of Edinburgh work behind the scenes to resolve problems that mainstream society is not willing to accept. Just because people don't accept the problem it doesn't mean it doesn't exist. Magic still infuses the lives of everyone, but people don't always notice. It might be that they are too busy to allow themselves to experience wonder, or that they are now too good at excluding things from their thoughts which don't fit into their world view.

The clues are there if you are looking properly. It could be the shadow that moves without reason, but you ignore it as a trick of the light, or maybe that you are too tired. The sparkle of light you see from the corner of your eye that is probably just a reflection of light from a passing car.

These could just be what they seem, minor errors of perception or they could be the hidden world impinging upon the mundane. It takes an open mind to believe there might be something happening. It takes skill to truly know the difference.

A modern Witch is no longer used for curing cattle, unless they now also work as a vet. We are no longer feared as the dreaded crone who can cast the evil eye out of spite. We have seamlessly merged into the normal mass of people. Integrated. Hidden in plain sight.

We watch, and wait, and when you need one of us, we will be there. Even if you don't know them, at the right time if you are lucky, they will know you.

We wait for those times when the dark reaches out, those times when the people lose their way. All Witches watch and wait, guardians and denizens of the boundaries.

Bridget

The muted buzzing from my pocket only slowly penetrated into my contemplation of the patient's file I was reading. The intricacies of what to try next for this patient was taxing me, I had tried the simple things, now we might have to refer them on to get help. I rubbed my eyes with one hand as I reached with the other into the jacket that I had draped over the back of my chair. The narrow cut of the pocket frustrated my one handed attempt so I had to stand to get the phone out, it was thankfully still ringing by the time I managed to answer it.

I didn't recognise the number and it wasn't anyone already in my phone book. I guarded this number jealously so it wasn't likely a cold call, although it might be a wrong number. I checked the clock on the wall. I had a few minutes. Presented with the mystery I decided that there was an easy way to find out who it was. There is nothing worse for me than not knowing something. A ringing phone left unanswered grates on my nerves.

Curious about where this might lead I pushed the button and said a polite but questioning "Hello".

"Ermm, Hi, is that Bridget?" Almost instantly the nervous tone of voice of the caller made me aware that what followed was going to be excruciatingly embarrassing for the person on the other end of the phone.

As he knew my name it was definitely not a wrong number. I carefully schooled myself so I didn't laugh out loud, even if it turned out to be as ridiculous as I feared.

Anyone using this number during the working day, and sounding like this man did, was clearly someone deeply in need. Glancing to double check the clock, I gauged how much time I had between patients. A last minute no-show and sheer blind luck meant I had a couple of minutes to spare for a change. If I believed in miracles that would have been marked down as one. The next patient was a puzzle to solve in person once they arrived.

"Hi, yes, this is Bridget. What can I do for you?" I could feel the edges of my lips turning upwards into a slight smile. It was the only sign I permitted myself that my intrigued amusement was growing. I ensured that my tone was measured and clear. Not allowing any hint of my feelings to bleed through into my voice.

After years of practice I knew, and had been told, that I sounded calm and receptive. The epitome of modern professional practice. I was the image of the NHS at its caring best, from our wood & chrome offices to our calm and caring staff. Appearances are very important.

The truth is often more disturbing to people than a polite lie. What most people don't realise is that underneath that surface, at least in my case, lies a good solid layer of old fashioned Schadenfreude.

It is not thought of as an attractive trait but is very much a professional hazard for those working within the medical community.

Or perhaps a perk, depending on how you look at it. I am good at keeping it well hidden. But it is there and only very rarely has the mask slipped when I was where a patient could see.

"My name's John, I seem … to be having a … slight problem." He paused, the doubt and worry in his tone of voice were emphasised by his hesitancy.

It didn't take any magical training to tell that the British sense of understatement was definitely at play. Certain turns of phrase are warning flags for other people who don't like to make a scene, even if in reality 'a scene' might actually be warranted.

The self effacing nature of the term 'slight problem' was probably covering an emotional trauma on the scale of an amputated arm. It just needed to be translated out of the polite phrasing into the messy reality. If he had said the situation was 'pretty sticky' I would have tried to arrange to see him immediately.

"Maebh thought you might be able to help me. She gave me your number."

This was going to be a good one. All the clues were there. There was a very slightly panicked undertone to the voice, it was all in the uneven rush and slight stumble of the delivery. The conflict he was feeling and wasn't able to articulate meant this was something significant, even if he was downplaying it at this stage of the conversation.

"Can we meet up and discuss this, I think I'm going crazy as it is. And I don't want to just sound like a loony on the phone. Maebh said you would understand. She said that you would be able to … help" I was definitely intrigued. I looked at the clock again and mentally rehearsed my afternoon schedule.

"Look, I'm busy up until after five thirty today, but I could maybe meet you for a coffee just after six?" I wanted to make this easy for him.

I would have to have been devoid of sense to miss that he was in need. But he was still in fear and so hesitant that if I had been anything other than welcoming he could be easily scared off. All it would take is the wrong emphasis on a word and he might run off. Whatever had generated both this level of genuine nervous embarrassment about his mild fear for his sanity, and had made Maebh give him my number, would be worth finding out more about.

"That's great. How about the big café on George IV Bridge, near the library, you know the one? Is that okay?" I could almost see him slump on the other end of the phone as the relief in his voice was that palpable. Never before had my bland acceptance of a suggested meeting been received so gratefully. John quickly became effusive. "That's great. Thank you! See you later."

Hanging up my phone I went to put it away and struggled to get it back into my jacket pocket, as it was draped over the chair.

My phone was an old small thing. It only did calls, and texts at a push. Maebh teased me about being a 'Luddite' but I was happier without all the bells and whistles. Despite its comparatively small size it still managed to be cumbersome for fitting into my jacket's pockets if the angle wasn't perfect. I wondered if it was one of those style versus practicality things.

This sartorial inequality was a source of deep frustration for me that women were so often deprived of having useful pockets in so many items of clothing. It struck to the heart of my practical nature that something so simple was made inaccessible for no good reason. Maybe I should find a tailor?

Pushing that minor frustration aside my thoughts returned to the mystery man on the phone. I couldn't help but mutter to myself "I wonder what it is going to be this time?"

Maebh wasn't going to hand over my number for anything simple. It wasn't going to be a little bit of more discrete medical help for something that he was too embarrassed to see this regular GP about. She knew better than to try and involve me with problems of that nature. There were now clinics that handled that sort of thing, with more confidentiality than can sometimes be achieved in a small community practice. If Maebh had referred him to me because of its complications, they were guaranteed to be reasonably complicated.

His fear of sounding insane reinforced this as something that fell into the unbelievable category. It would be due to what I sometimes thought of as my other speciality. Not something that was covered in standard GP training. I began to think over potential situations that would lead to him feeling insane, but with enough doubt that it wasn't just a simple psychiatric problem. Maebh must have seen something in him.

Shortly afterwards the tell-tale buzz told me it was time to step out to fetch my next patient, and the comparatively straightforward medical help of my day job. There were still a couple of hours until I would be free to pursue my own projects, and if he was willing to wait then so could I. For now.

It was quite nice to be able to savour the prospect of a problem at a distance. I regard myself as a bit of a connoisseur when it came to tricky problems, and like anyone with the penchant for a challenge, part of the joy is always in the anticipation.

******

The afternoon went by in the normal blur of activity and administration. The final duties of making sure all the records were updated and any additional bits filed took up the last chunk of my time. Necessary but never exciting. While I do love my job it was with a mild sense of relief that I finally stepped out of the air-conditioned environment of the GPs' surgery. Something I knew my colleagues held as an unusual luxury, but it never sat quite right with me.

Stopping for a second to deeply breathe in the air of the warm summer evening. I always took this important moment of spiritual decompression. It was my first point of transition.

On the surface I work hard to present the perfect image of a respectable 21st century Edinburgh GP. It is a matter of personal choice. I ensure I am always smartly dressed in a stylish yet sober suit, with the skirt respectably just covering my knees. I keep my hair tightly constrained in a bun. I maintain this 'professional' appearance as a vital smokescreen to keeping my patients' trust. It helps if you can make use of their willingness not to question things if presented with a plausible story.

The reason for the elaborate smokescreen is that underneath the surface the truth was much more complicated.

I am a Witch as well as a GP. This duality to my existence has made things difficult sometimes.

I am uncomfortable as the hidden truth does not fit neatly into the pattern of conformity that is the social norm for people in my profession.

To a certain extent this façade-building is common for people with my job. Nearly everyone has a work persona but not all of them are hiding something quite as arcane as being a Witch. Nonetheless I take some comfort from the fact that there are plenty of other people who live more than one life between office and home, even if that second life is not literally magical.

It was this double life that had, without much struggle or taxing of brains, given birth to the playful nickname that some people use behind my back. To them I am the 'Witch Doctor'. There are a few people who use it and think I don't know, but I let them. It works. It is true. Despite the amused wink that sometimes goes with it, there is also enough respect in their voices that I allow it to continue.

If I felt they were just taking the mickey I would have had to put a stop to it quickly. I may have my secrets but respect is an important tool, and that sort of mockery would not be tolerated. Some people thrive on the respect of others, their standing in the community is part of who they are. This applies strongly to Witches, even those who operate mostly in secret.

Respect is vital. Given the hurdle of being skilled at something people didn't believe in anymore, being disrespected on top of that is intolerable.

I feel quite pleased with myself I am certain that none of the patients in my day job suspect that I am anything other than a standard middle class Edinburgher. I believe that I have successfully kept people from suspecting there is anything going on that is worth discussing over scones in any Edinburgh teashop.

If nothing else I liked that I was not an open book to everyone. I have never been comfortable with people knowing all of my business, and have deflected some indirect enquiries from little old ladies that I am sure would have impressed professional interrogators. They were not pleased but I managed to remain a bit mysterious.

As I walked away from the office it was time for the next bit of my ritual decompression. I pulled out the ornate pin that held my hair up in the tight bun. It helped me mark the transition from my work life to my personal one. This was a small psychological switch that helped me to relax. As I pulled it out there was a physical release of tension throughout my entire body.

As my hair spilled down around my shoulders I was able to feel the last traces of the staid work persona fall away. I genuinely hate being so constrained, but I choose it as a necessary sacrifice to maintain the façade I feel that is expected of me. The mask I have learnt to wear.

There had been that uncomfortable period during the transition from university to the working world when I discovered the downside of individuality in my field of work. People trade on reputation. I quickly noted that the more 'eccentric' people were sidelined. Even the highly skilled ones.

On one hand I can see how it helps people trust you by having a standard doctor template, for appearance and character. Nonetheless on the other it made me sad that people felt this was necessary. Disconnection from the varied experiences and characters that make up our world is sustained as the unquestioned norm.

It is part of a wider problem. It is all linked, this drive for a form of disconnected simplicity. People would rather have a machine to keep information, rather than remembering things or writing them down. They want another machine for cooling the air, rather than opening the window.

Ironically I think that rather than being more simple it makes complications abound when people try to 'make' things better. It is the easy lie rather than the uncomfortable truth. The world is messy and people are part of that world.

I looked at my watch and gauged that I was possibly a little late so I picked up my pace a little. The light breeze teasing my hair out as I strode felt pleasurable. Simultaneously helping to loosen the last few knots in my mind and put work thoughts behind me. Literally letting my hair down, allows me to feel free and get into the space where I can express my inner Witch.

"Simpler is better." I muttered. Talking to myself in public was a habit I knew I should break, in case I said something I shouldn't at the wrong time. I had been doing it since I was a child and had so far proven completely intractable.

Ordinarily I love the fact that I am not 'normal' and that I am quite unique in some of my views. I had however decided that until I had safely navigated the precarious early stages of my career and established myself properly in a practice that this was going to be concealed. My individuality is very important to me, but so is making a living, and paying bills.

Despite my best efforts there are a few people I knew professionally, those who spend a bit more time with me, that have picked up a vibe that I am a little outside of the 'mainstream'. Even if they can't pin down exactly what it was that made them feel that way. My secret remains safe so far.

Beyond those astute colleagues who have a nagging feeling that I am a little unusual, maybe a little eccentric, but not too eccentric, I was on the whole able to present a convincing illusion of normality. The talking to myself was going to take a lot more work to fix. Luckily so far it hadn't caused many problems.

The only silver lining in all this was that looking back on my years at university there were definitely some of my now colleagues in the medical school who were determined to redefine the boundaries of 'quirky'. So I was able to appear completely normal, at least by comparison.

Sadly that context wasn't quite as secure in Edinburgh.

Although I had fallen in love with the place, it had been chosen for me by circumstances. It was now my home and where I was needed. However the city was a lot more stuffy than what I had been used to before.

As an aspiring GP I feel I have to 'conform' a lot more than I would choose. Looking around I think the people who made up the 'establishment' of the city were still a little too constrained and old school Presbyterian, and by that meaning Knoxian, to accept that one of the supposed 'Pillars of the Community' might not be a "good", and by that meaning a "fundamentally boring", person.

It is a sad truth that, on the whole, society prefers it that the people with any type of power aren't too interesting. The history of most political scandals is about the revelation that the person in power is a more flawed and complicated individual than previously suspected.

This can happen even if the area of their life being exposed has no bearing on the actual execution of their duties, it still never ends well for them.

I took this lesson from history to heart and did my best to keep up a good front. Deflection and misdirection have become second nature to me. I am not the first person who has evolved these simple defence mechanisms. It is designed to not tax the tolerance of those who could inconvenience me if they had a mind to, just through stubborn disapproval. Across the world prejudice of all sorts sadly permeates into decisions often without the person being aware, and life is tough enough.

The old attitudes are changing, but these things take time. The scale of my secret might even make the most open minded person pause in shock.

So I make sure that any hint of Witchcraft, even the more mainstream end is kept hidden. Not a pentagram nor triple moon in sight. I had seen children comment on a stranger's tattoo asking 'why the lady had a sweetie on her arm'.

The disapproval in the expression of the parent was enough to reinforce my decision to keep that part of my life quiet.

This may sound paranoid but over the years I have seen reflected in the eyes of the some of the more staunchly religious, or socially conservative, people the banked but still smouldering fires of the Witch burnings. Sadly not yet completely extinguished.

Anyone with ears can hear the impassioned denunciations from pulpits or secular soapboxes about what is viewed as 'normal' and what is deemed 'acceptable'. This sort of proclamation is never too far from the lips of those holding back the tide of change, the ones who see their privilege and power eroding as the playing field levels.

Thankfully there are also those who feel less threatened by the process, attempting to help it along despite the other group's protestations. Edinburgh was a good place for change, just not necessarily a fast one.

Shaking my head to clear these thoughts I was tempted to pause for a moment and enjoy the view out across the open green expanse. The beautiful vista of Bruntsfield Links and the Meadows always cheered my heart but my appointment kept me walking.

There is something special about being able to see the towering extinct volcano of Arthur's Seat that sits in the middle of the city. It makes me feel pleased that this is now my adopted home, although I sometimes wonder if I adopted it, or it adopted me.

I realised that my thoughts about my own situation were just an echo of the concerns that I had heard over the phone earlier. Those suppressed feelings and thoughts. Where I was now going to delve into someone else's own version of that. My meeting with this mysterious John.

The puzzle of the 'non-standard' problems that were brought to me on occasion were always much more challenging than the daily tasks I face as a local GP. They always hold that extra frisson of excitement. There is a sense of satisfaction I get from helping people in normal ways, and wouldn't give up even if I could.

There are two sides to the world, the mundane and the fantastical but both are equally real. I feel it is important to remember that and doing the normal work keeps me grounded. Witches who forgot the boundaries were prone to end up starring in the sorts of tales that don't end well for them. However the 'occult', and by that I really do mean hidden, aspects of my life are just that much more exciting.

As I started to ponder on what sort of problem this stranger might be bringing to me I began to feel a shift in the air. There was a sudden drop in temperature. I looked up wondering if it might just be a cloud crossing the sun, but the sky was clear.

Allowing my senses to tune into the sensation I discovered the chill was accompanied by the very unseasonal smell of snow and pine trees. It passed almost instantly but I could tell something was out of kilter.

Winter was trying to make its presence felt in late July. This is unusual even in Scotland. I felt the muscles in my face tighten as I couldn't repress my concern. A disruption like that was obviously a herald of something more significant. 'I'll have to pay attention to this', I muttered, rubbing my arms to counteract the last of the brief chill that had touched my skin.

I tried to work out what this might mean, but despite all my best efforts the Sight has never been my strongest skill within the craft. All that happened was this erratic moment of insight just left me feeling worried and on my guard, but with no idea from what. I have always found the vagaries of fortune telling just frustrating. There were always too many options until after it was known and by then it was too late. Despite appreciating those who were able to navigate these visions I found it much easier, even in my magical work to deal with the here and now. I decided that analysing this portent would take too much time so I pushed it from my mind and hurried onwards to ensure I would be on time for my new 'patient'.

The streets and buildings of the outskirts of Edinburgh's Old Town engulfed me as I picked up my pace, navigated the busy Tollcross junction. I passed swiftly through one of the less salubrious areas of town where the stag nights tended to congregate. Nestled within spitting distance of the Town's financial area and in the shadow of the Castle.

I reflected briefly on the mass of contradictions that made up Edinburgh, a staunchly moral surface establishment that thrived with a strong undercurrent of other 'less moral' establishments and goings on.

Knowing my history I was familiar with this idea that this other world often kept things ticking over behind the scenes. One couldn't seem to exist without the other, a duality that defied reformation. The reminder that people are at their heart neither irredeemable sinners nor perfect saints.

"Things never change" I muttered as I continued on my path by cutting down through the Grassmarket to arrive nearly directly underneath my destination. Looking up from the lower level of the overlapping roads that make up Edinburgh I found myself wishing again that I could be more blasé and use my powers to do something impressive. I repressed the urge as I realised that Edinburgh, or to be fair the modern world, was not ready to embrace the idea of a flying woman in broad daylight. Night time however was a different matter altogether.

Under cover of darkness I had dabbled on occasion. The temptation of that particular skill was great but also came with a significant risk, other than that of discovery. The more impressive the feat of magic the higher the price tag. Flying for example required yourself to be nearly completely open to the underlying energy of the world. To make yourself part of that flow while still controlling your direction and the connection to it and the integrity of your body. It is highly addictive. If used too frequently your connection to the mundane reality can suffer.

Putting to one side my risky urge I turned right and made the necessary slog up Candlemaker Row to get to the right level of the city. Tourists often got confused about this particular foible of Edinburgh's topography, there are occasionally people who will arrange to meet at the junction of George IV Bridge and the Cowgate. However unless they could hover 30 feet in the air they were on a hiding to nothing with that plan. You would think the word 'Bridge' would give them a clue.

As I reached the top of the hill, the temperature dropped suddenly again. Even though the air was still it came as a ghostly sensation of cold wind cutting through the previously balmy summer air. Without stirring even a single hair on my head. The chill striking to the bone, and just as suddenly gone. Whatever I had picked up a strand of on the Links was getting more intense.

I looked around from this new vista searching for some other outward sign, the closest I could get was the odd behaviour of a single grey cloud. Not particularly overwhelming as a portent, it was just a dark smudge against a bright summer sky. It was hovering over the bridge and trying to look threatening, but, being quite small it did not quite manage it.

I felt a sudden surge of irritation at myself, looking for portents in a cloud. Unless there were a lot more of them it couldn't pose any real threat. The stillness of it bothered me, there was something amiss, but I wasn't able to define it. There wasn't anything I could do without more information so I went forward, my patient awaited.

Putting my head down I progressed along George IV Bridge and approached the now much more famous coffee Shop. I slowed slightly to ensure that I was looking as professional as I could be, despite having shifted into my off duty mode. I wanted to make the right first impression. I needed to be both a doctor and a witch.

I paused briefly to smooth my hair and straighten my jacket in the hazy reflection provided by the large window of the café.

Every time I came here I fondly recalled the amusement that I felt when they had briefly displayed a sign saying 'The Birthplace of Harry Potter – Now Selling Draught Beers'. The incongruity of the conjunction of a children's character and an alcohol sales notice had shocked me a little, but after a little reflection and some quick mental arithmetic of a fictional character's age I had conceded at the time "Well I suppose he is of drinking age now." I don't know if anyone had complained, or if the staff had swiftly realised that this was not the best sign they had ever commissioned and removed it.

Having made myself a bit more presentable for my appointment I crossed the threshold of the café. Instantly I did so my senses heightened but this combined with the disconcerting effect that things felt as if they were trying to go out of focus at the same time. It reminded me slightly of being drunk but it was not accompanied by any pleasant feelings of relaxation.

Despite all this confusion it came to me that all doors serve as liminal zones, they mark off one thing from another. I had definitely crossed some sort of line. It was clear that something wasn't right here, but I felt drawn onwards.

A small part of my mind was trying to express that maybe stopping was the best plan. My feet and the rest of my instincts were out voting it and so natural caution was ignored and curiosity lead the way.

My hair, despite my last minute neatening, was already beginning to feel like it was trying to stand straight out from my head. My skin was also prickling, not just my thumbs. There was definitely a field of some sort of energy, but it was nothing so banal as static electricity.

The other patrons of the café seemed entirely oblivious that anything out of the ordinary was going on. The normal chat and clatter continued around me but sounded too loud and distorted. My sense of unreality was increasing, with echoes of bad dreams.

Reaching the corner and entering the space at the back which opened out for more tables I felt the power surge. My vision darkened for a second as if I had stood up too quickly, but this was no simple case of temporary hypotension. What I had done was locate the source of the energy disturbance. He was an attractive but slightly built man, with dark hair and an honest looking face.

He was anxiously watching everyone who came round the corner, but trying not to be too obvious about it at the same time – obviously British.

He stood up quickly as I approached and stepped forward, moving confidently and lightly. Even if he wasn't who I was here to meet I was feeling drawn to him as inevitably as a swimmer in a rip tide. Despite my altered state I couldn't help but notice he was very graceful, carrying himself with an athletic poise.

I stopped as he began to approach me, the disorientation of the power making it impossible for me to move forward. Even though the power surging around me was overwhelming it was not accompanied by any feeling of threat. I am not normally one to calmly accept powerlessness, but in that moment, it was not an unpleasant sensation. I watched curiously from within, gauging what was happening. Waiting to see how this developed. It was all just too odd to quantify, so I bided my time.

John

I hung up the phone and sighed. It had been easier than I hoped, she had sounded very professional on the phone. But now it was all feeling very real. I done the thing, now I had to wait. I looked at my room which I was currently finding quite depressing. I had been straightening up everything to within an inch of its life. My neatly bed made. The books both neatened and alphabetised.

Everything was in perfect order. Perfect, boring, order.

There was nothing left to do. Normally I lived in what I had heard called 'hobo chic', that lived-in look that came from just going out and doing things most of the time. I thought it had a bit of character. Or a bloody mess as my parents used to call it. That was normally. Things weren't normal at the moment and that is why everything was neat. I hoped it would help me, tidying up would distract me. But instead it had made it worse, the mess had normally hidden the uninspired décor that was the pragmatic bedrock of a rental property.

It wasn't bad, it was just that it left me looking at death by manilla mediocrity.

I sat and looked at what I had done. The blandness and tidiness made me feel worse. It made the room feel smaller. As if I were trapped in a prison cell.

The feeling of claustrophobia that seemed to be stemming from this was not helped by the reality of flat sharing. There is an unnatural compression of having all your possessions crammed into one room.

Frustrated by it all I went to stand at the window. Maybe there would be an interesting cloud, or something. Anything. I was quite lucky with the view here, being on the top floor of the tenement gave me some pretty cool views.

I looked out over the patchwork of trees, walls and small other odds and sods that made up the back green behind my building. Normally the pocket of nature giving a touch of wildness and colour to the orderly limits of the buildings made me smile, the cosy harmony between nature and civilisation. Now it felt wrong. It wasn't enough. It looked pathetic and sad, an echo of wildness caged. It reminded me of the inside space that lacked any spark of life. It felt hollow. I watched the shadows of the trees far below.

As I stared at them a memory came back to me. I was standing on a mountain top looking down at a wild landscape. There was no sign of anything human. No roads, not even an electricity pylon. It felt such a real memory, but I couldn't remember ever having been anywhere like that. I wondered if it was from a movie, but part of it was the cold wind biting my face. I could also feel the land below me. It was alive. It was a tingling in my whole body that was strongest in my feet.

The memory made me feel a little dizzy, but it was also good. Alive. It came with the knowledge that there weren't any people. The birds were alone in the sky, the water was fresh and pure. It was all peace and wildness. I closed my eyes and let the memory fill me up. The tingling started again. Until the scream came.

I jerked and opened my eyes. It was a fire engine. Just a normal everyday sound. The tingling changed into anger. It became a fire that swept through me. I wanted to level the city. Civilisation had crushed the beauty from the world. The forests had been burned, nature had been destroyed. It felt right that someone should bring it back. I just needed to work out how to make it happen. It would be easy if the trees were encouraged.

Roots can easily tear through concrete. I felt pain in my hands and realised I had clenched them into fists, my nails digging into the skin of my hands. My heart was racing. I stopped myself.

That was dangerous thinking, it was like I was channelling a super villain. Pulling myself together I pushed those feelings deep down. Getting angry felt wrong but it was at least understandable, unlike the rest of what had been happening this week.

Still I was fairly certain that plotting cataclysmic destruction of a city was not a reasonable thing to find yourself doing on a Friday afternoon. Filing the thought away in the 'bad idea' category I was able to go back to worrying about how much of a mess I was at the moment. It was becoming a familiar one, but uncomfortable.

To distract myself I looked down at my arm sticking out from my shirt. The muscles there were still in good condition. Starting with my hand I tensed them in groups moving up my arm and then cascaded that sensation down my body.

It felt good as they responded to my commands. They at least were in working order. It was just my mind that wasn't feeling quite so good. And I wasn't sure how to handle it.

My emotional well-being had gone from being something that I didn't need to worry about to something that was overwhelming me and refusing to respond to reason and self discipline. I hadn't been able to find the words for what was happening, so I lied. It was much simpler that way.

This was my second day off work. I had felt such a mess Wednesday night and had barely slept that it made calling in sick very easy, and I even sounded convincing. I had told them I was coming down with a summer flu. I found it easy to justify the lie, I knew I wasn't just skiving off work. I really was ill. It was just not something as simple as a cold. I had after a bit of a struggle admitted I was genuinely not capable of concentrating.

It was difficult for me to acknowledge the probable cause but was able to admit that there was definitely something wrong. I was caught in a logical loop that I wasn't able to step out of. I didn't feel it but I was probably completely insane. It is not a comforting conclusion to reach. Given the potential consequences of showing up at a hospital and having to explain to them that I thought I might be insane, it was not a step I wanted to rush. So, to give myself time to think and engage in that age-old struggle of self versus self, I did what anyone would and procrastinated.

Having been given a new option and making the call I felt a bit better. With time to think I went over how long I had been putting it off. It was bizarre how things had happened. Yesterday a few hours after I had called in sick, there had been a knock at my door. It was Maebh. She was at best a fun, casual, acquaintance. She had somehow tracked me down and hadn't wanted to take no for an answer when I tried saying I wasn't feeling up to visitors.

She had persuaded me to let her in. In fact I had nearly dragged her in when she started talking more loudly on the doorstep about what she had seen happen the previous night. I was doing my best to forget about it. She really didn't look like she was going to just go away. She began to ask me all sorts of questions. It was really odd and she often paused and looked like she was listening intently to the silence when I had stopped talking. I did my best to not tell her anything, to try and hide it as I found her intensity a bit off putting.

After a while she began to make hints that she felt there something 'unusual' going on that she felt I might need help with. She tried offering to see what she could do, and I quickly refused. It was making me feel more uncomfortable and I was starting to think she might be just as crazy as I was.

I began rambling about wondering which hospital it was best that I go to, as it felt too dramatic to try and get an ambulance. She interrupted me, obviously exasperated. She said "I have a better idea for you. I know just the Doctor you should see. My friend the Witch Doctor!"

It was so ridiculous I almost laughed in her face. Why would anyone call themselves that? She quickly reassured me that what she was suggesting was a meeting with an actual qualified GP.

Just one Maebh promised would have the required additional skills that I apparently needed. The idea of a Witch Doctor played on my mind for a bit.

I had some odd mental images that I realised came from Bettlegeuse, possibly seen at too young an age, but which made me think about shrunken heads and creative uses of bones for personal adornments. I quickly realised that these were both highly unlikely for an Edinburgh GP and also a bit culturally insensitive so I did my best to focus on what Maebh was saying. While initially shocked it took hold and I wanted to learn more.

She spent another half an hour telling me that this Bridget would be able to help me. She reassured me that I was just overreacting and shouldn't rush into anything. Once she was no longer trying to help me herself I relaxed a bit more and she was very persuasive on behalf of this Bridget.

She seemed sympathetic but I just didn't feel able to trust her. There was a certain sharpness about her sometimes that made me reluctant to tell her anything more than she had already seen. She assured me that Bridget would see me privately so I didn't have to go into a normal surgery and explain what I thought was happening.

The potential embarrassment had been a major factor in my unwillingness to deal with what was happening. Honesty, in the face of likely ridicule, was more brave than I felt able to muster at that point. So Maebh's lifeline, as unlikely as it sounded, was the less bad option.

I finally got Maebh to leave by agreeing that I would call Bridget. What harm could come from meeting this woman for a coffee and seeing what she had to say about things. If she was as good as Maebh said and could see to the heart of things easily, I might not have to actually say anything.

Despite my reluctance to confide in her I could now see why people tended to do what she told them. I couldn't help but wonder if she was also a Witch but I had decided that I didn't want to ask her outright. I wasn't sure if it was polite or not. It might be like asking a Canadian "which part of the States are you from?" and other such mistakes. After she left I sat with the telephone number in my hand and thought about when I would make the call.

I began to rehearse what I would say. I still had to struggle with myself to put the situation into words that I was comfortable saying. It was all just a bit too crazy. I had struggled a bit when Maebh had gone on about "overcoming my heteronormative conditioning" and "facing up" to my emotions.

I must admit I normally preferred not dealing with my emotions as they tended to be messy and cause more problems than they solved.

Pretending all was fine and avoiding situations where anyone was likely to cry suited me a lot better. However I was now coming to realise that this was not working for me at the moment. I had to consider something new.

Now that I thought about it, Maebh showing up had been quite useful as it helped me to realise that I had been attempting to come up with a rational cause for the events of the last few days. I had been stuck on what I felt was a reasonable but potentially misleading question. If you can ask if you are insane does it probably mean that you aren't?

It wasn't unreasonable for me to be reluctant to decide that I had spontaneously developed a serious psychiatric disorder. Even though it was looking like the most plausible explanation.

I had difficulty in facing up to the potential consequences of this and it was only partly based on my fear of having it confirmed. There was a certain element of how it felt un-British to willingly go into that tooth-grindingly embarrassing situation of admitting openly that something was seriously wrong.

The most difficult thing for me to reconcile in the entire process was that while it was so obviously illogical, but it all felt genuine. There is only so far you can go with "I know this will sound entirely insane but..." and I hadn't quite gotten to that point yet.

I decided to sleep on it and see if I felt more courage the next day. Part of me hoped that maybe I would be feeling better and none of this would matter anymore.

I then did my best to try and spend as normal an evening as possible. It was then that I had begun the tidying up of my room that was now making me so depressed. Like so many things it had seemed like a good idea at the time.

After I had tidied up I made a light dinner; as I sat down to eat I was caught by the change in the quality of light, one of the perks of big windows in these old houses. I was drawn to look out into the peaceful evening. It had been a glorious evening and I was suffused with a feeling of peace. I just stood there enjoying looking out across the town. The way that the late summer's evening glow made everything it touched look soft and warm. I was filled with a deep contentment at the sight of the world in obvious harmony with itself. It is astounding how a change in mood can alter a reaction to the same view.

I had put most of my thoughts about Maebh's visit from my head while I was tidying, but in that moment of calm I felt it surface again and something clicked into place. I was caught between two parts of myself, the romantic and the practical.

The loudest voice in my head was the one that kept me on the steady path. The one that suggested that maybe this GP, even if she was also a witch, would just give me some pills to make the strangeness go away. It would keep things simple.

It was the other voice, the one I normally ignored, that while 'strange' was different: it was just another term for unfamiliar. Every friend starts as a stranger.

In the calm that I found I realised that only a year or so ago, there were a lot of things in my current life that I would have regarded as more than strange. A few things, and a few of my new friends, would have been seen as downright weird.

A year can be a long time, if you do a lot with it. It had been just over a year ago when I moved to Edinburgh and had learned a few new things about the world. More importantly I had worked out things about myself that I hadn't allowed myself to know before. In my old life I really had no clue that there was more to this world than work, the pub, and the other normal daily things that everyone shares. The same television shows, the sporting triumphs, or defeats, depending on who you supported. These normal but unremarkable things that made the news were what had been how I understood the world.

I now realised, as trite as it sounded, that I had opened my eyes. It felt weird to me now that most people thought it was normal to go around not looking more than a few inches from the well-worn path of standard mediocrity.

It was like everyone is wearing an invisible set of blinkers. They don't notice that there is more to life than what they have pointed themselves towards. Despite these lessons I still didn't feel confident that I was entirely sane, but in those moments of insight I felt fully entitled to my self-righteousness. I had managed to change my view, so why couldn't everyone else do the same!

The practical part of my brain kicked in and pointed out to me that it had only been a short time before that I had been exactly like them. It had been the people I met that had opened me up, rather than any personal journey of discovery that I had set myself on. All it took was a chance encounter at a party that had brought new people into my life. It was these new people, sharing their own experiences with me that had opened up my horizons. Without this experience I would not have had enough perspective to reach this current revelation. It was all down to Jeff.

He had just been a cool guy at a party who had been up for a chat with a stranger, and who had then introduced me to a different world. One that existed alongside the normal one I lived in. Through him, and his friends, I learnt about a different way of thinking and started hanging out with a new group of people.

The odd thing about this lot was that they got together on a regular basis to mark the old Celtic pagan fire festivals. They did this with performances and bonfires, and more than a little partying, which is unsurprising as these, were traditionally times to celebrate fertility. The parties were the main thing that got my attention, but the other stuff, once I got over how weird it sounded actually really appealed to me.

The transition had not entirely been smooth. Blinkers are quite comfortable things. Once I began to get over myself, I realised that there was a lot to appreciate about the world.

Diversity is actually pretty cool once you get over the shock. Some of them had chosen standard paths, but a lot were seeking new ways to exist. Ways that met their personal needs and didn't just reflect what would have been the easy pattern for them to follow. There were some very out-there thinkers in the society, but on the whole were good people who just wanted to express themselves. Even if that didn't match the categories that other people expected.

As I thought about the last few months, it was not as if I had kept on with the normal limits. Just a few short months ago I had been up there with them. Marking Beltane. Getting into the spirit of the festival, and enjoying the thought that the Summer was well and truly on its way. The concepts of growth and change were really appealing ideas.

Working in an office all day had reinforced my disconnection from nature. I used to love being outdoors as a kid, but before getting involved with Beltane I couldn't remember when I had previously, as an adult, last been out into a forest. Or walked along a beach just to hear the surf or feel the wind off the sea. Now I was part of it. It was nice to get closer to nature.

Thinking back to the night itself, I closed my eyes briefly to recall the sight of the gyrating painted bodies of the reds. The flames of the torches flickering in the winds up the hill just reinforced the primal and chaotic feeling.

The beats of the drums added to the excitement. I could smell the paraffin in the air again. The memory felt so strong it was like I was back there, the happiness was growing inside me. The stirring of my desire I recalled from the night started again. It felt good. I let myself linger on that thought for a little while. The ache began to hurt so I pushed it away. I wanted to be back there. Now. Part of it all again. That was impossible so I let the feeling go and turned to head to my bed.

As I looked around an unexpected flash of colour caught my eye. The peace lily I had been given as a gift by the Whites was sitting on the shelf near me, and amongst the white blossoms I noticed a new one. A red one. I went and had a closer look, and it seemed natural. I would have to ask them if this was a special species that could change colours. It seemed oddly apt, but the ebbing emotions now that I had pushed them down left me feeling utterly exhausted. Wanting to try and get a proper night's sleep for a change, I continued on to my bed. The flower would just be another thing to work out tomorrow.

I was out of luck. It felt that as soon as I closed my eyes I was back on the Hill. The previous daydream I had tried to suppress had been strong, but this was even more real. I could feel the chill of the air in sharp contrast to my bare, body painted, skin. I knew it was cold but it didn't bother me. I could feel the heat radiating out of me. It was echoed back to me by the bodies of the reds.

The occasional flare of flame felt cool compared to my body. The spectators were there but were about as substantial as ghosts, an indistinct blur marking a line.

I was there again. In that moment.

I slowly walked around the stage. My eyes fixed on the May Queen.

Around us the Reds ran and the Whites span in opposing circles, to the crescendo of the drums, throbbing through us all. She looked so seductive in her pale innocence. Turning just out of my reach. I stalked her, moving in the opposite direction. Not making eye contact, but seeking out her face on each rotation. I felt the connection between us deepen again.

The tide of the rhythm replacing my heart beat with an external source. The sound became the world. My need to touch her growing with each passing flash of her face. I still held back. The body in front of me almost fluorescing in the flickering fire. I felt my body burn with the heat to echo her flame. I still held back. The moment slowed. The movements I made felt glacial and her rotation became that of the distant moon. I knew it was the moment.

Our eyes met. My hand crossed the light years that separated us. The memory unfolded. I knew what I was now expecting. The firm but yielding contact of my hand upon a body. Instead as I touched her, the May Queen exploded into light and a searing pain flashed up my arm and through my body. It wrenched a scream from my throat as I felt my body dissolve under the force of the energy I had just received. It was the pain of being destroyed by that which you sought to possess.

My loss hurt more as I also knew I had failed at the moment of potential victory. I felt myself disappear in that flash of defeated knowledge.

I woke trembling.

My bedclothes clung to me as I was dripping with sweat. The ache from the dream lingered. My entire body felt like I had been scalded down to the bone. I shook myself to try and get rid of the feeling of the dream. Maybe I really did have the flu and this was the fever finally appearing? If it was, I could hope that it would just need bed rest and fluids. All of the other stuff could be blamed on delusions brought on by a fever.

I wasn't sure if I had screamed out in real life, and after a moment of worry I was relieved to remember that Ewan was away. So no flatmate would be freaking out at me again. I wanted to just stay still but my throat felt parched so I decided to force myself out of bed. Water was necessary and no one else was going to get it for me. I swung my feet down and suddenly screamed again. This time in shock and revulsion. Quickly I brought my feet back up under the duvet, whatever they had touched had been moist and a bit spongy.

The logical part of my brain started suggesting that maybe the roof had leaked overnight, or the washing machine. I peeked over the edge of the bed to work out what I was dealing with.

The light was good, coming through a gap in my curtains. I could clearly see the moss that now covered a good two feet of the carpet surrounding my bed.

It was even starting to creep up the side of my bedside table. Just growing out of the carpet.

The logical part of my brain shut up at this point as it couldn't explain this one away. I lay back and started at the ceiling trying not to hyperventilate and waiting for the initial panic to pass.

Jumping and hopping over the moist moss so as not to have to re-experience the damp slimy feeling on my feet, I quickly grabbed my dressing gown and went to the kitchen to get a big black bin bag. As I began pulling it out of the carpet the moss began to die. The whole mass became very dry and crumbly in a matter of seconds. It didn't feel as bad, but I wanted to remove this very obvious clue that something very weird was happening. I dumped the bag out in the stairwell so I wouldn't have to look at it silently reminding me.

The only solution now was to have a sit-down and a cup of tea and work out what to say in my call to Bridget. It was only when I had this chance to sit and was cradling the tea that I realised how late it was. It was nearly lunch. The indoor gardening hadn't taken me that long, so I must have overslept quite significantly.

I cradled the hot cup in my hands and tried to allow it to calm me down a bit more while I thought through what I would say. It gave some reassurance but it was only holding back a little of the panic about having to face up to my potential insanity.

I tried to write down a few things to see if I could boil it all down to a few sentences. I discarded it all, the phone was not the right place for this.

I would just ask to meet her. As soon as possible. I started to dial, worried I had misdialed and hung up, changed my mind twice and after passing around I managed to finally make the call.

Waiting for her to pick up felt worse than when I had tried as a teenager to ask Sorrel Pinkerton out on a date to the pictures.

After I was done I sat and let myself go numb.

Glancing at my watch I realised I still had several hours to wait and nothing to focus on. Having set the ball in motion, I felt a bit flat and uncertain how to fill my time. I certainly didn't want to risk exploring any of the destructive ideas that had risen in his mind.

I briefly wondered if a bit of booze might help me get through until the afternoon, but I realised I ran the risk of overdoing it and either missing the appointment or making Bridget think I was just a crazy alcoholic. I decided the safest option was television. I normally didn't like it much but it was what I needed right now. The gentle numbing sensation of having non-challenging flickering images and overly simplistic views of the world acting as a bath for my brain would work.

It seemed to be good for leaching away any motivation to actually do anything. As long as he picked the boring programmes, and nothing well-written or provocative.

I had to suppress the resentment that I felt that I wasn't able to do anything else. Since getting involved in Beltane I had picked up some new skills, from some circus performer types who were connected to the wider community.

I was now a competent juggler with balls, and was getting better with bats, but I really liked doing the acrobatic stuff. It was a lot more satisfying than going to the gym which had been my previous main hobby, doing acro with people felt good. It was also better than just giving money to someone to help build muscle tone and lose body fat.

The problem was, for the last week or so I hadn't been able to stop easily if I started. My skills had been increasing rapidly which felt really good at first, but quickly I realised when training with other people I seemed to be driving too hard. The urge in my muscles was to do more, faster, stronger, for longer. Put in more effort, move more, keep going. It felt as if I had no upper limit anymore, I just wanted to do it forever, whatever it was. My zone had grown a lot.

I had begun to fantasise about juggling the moon, or doing acrobatics among the clouds. It had been harder and harder to stop every time. I had even hidden my juggling balls as they seemed to reproach me for not practising more, but I knew I couldn't handle another manic episode. Even just thinking about it made my fingers twitch, the temptation growing. I forced myself to sink deeper into the couch and just focus on the television and letting it wash over me.

The gradual shifting of the programmes from day-time offerings to the post-school fare signalled for me that the time was getting closer. I could feel my anxiety mounting. I had no idea what this Doctor was going to say to me.

Despite Maebh's reassurance that this was exactly Bridget's cup of tea, she had still been described as a serious doctor and so that left me with the feeling that I still might end up in a hospital in the near future. I tried to take confidence in the feeling that either way she was going to be able to help me.

As the time got closer I felt more and more physically uncomfortable, the clock seemed to be mocking me with how slowly it was moving. I decided it was time to head out instead. I hoped the act of walking would take my mind off of it.

I started working out the most convoluted route I could think of to waste the time that I still had to kill before my appointment. Despite my best efforts I still arrived just early enough to feel a bit ridiculous but without enough time to do anything other than head in.

Thinking about it, if I had made any more odd loops or pacing up and down outside would either make me risk being late, or make me seem a bit more obviously insane than I was happy to show off at this point. Weighing it all up I decided to head in and get myself a drink. I settled in to wait for my first appointment with the Witch Doctor.

I spent the next few minutes doing my best to be really subtle and low-key about seeing if the person coming around the corner was possibly Bridget arriving early. It felt really uncomfortable to be actually looking at a constant parade of strangers to try and recognise a strange woman who was going to help me.

I saw people giving me funny looks, and I realised I was getting more and more obvious as time went by. I wasn't sure what to do about it. The relief when someone who matched Maebh's description of Bridget perfectly came around the corner felt great. We had a connection like I had already met her, she was just so obviously Bridget. I jumped up to go and meet her on the way to the table and began to introduce myself.

I took her hand to shake it and felt a small static shock, and the sensation of knowing her got stronger. I was trying to work out where I might have seen her before when she suddenly seemed to be fainting. My acro training came in handy as I got hold of her arm and guided her into a nearby seat. It was like contact improvisation. She turned really pale and looked shaken.

I asked her how she was feeling, nearly thinking I could make a joke out it. Something along the lines of I don't normally have his affect on women, but the obvious shock on her face made me realise exactly how unhelpful that would be right then. After a few seconds she managed to whisper that she wanted some water so I went off to get it.

After I came back she was rubbing her hand as if it was stinging. She grabbed the water out of my hand and began to slowly sip it. I waved away the waitress who had followed me back. She looked concerned but I decided that Bridget would have asked for more definite help if she wanted it, so I sent her away.

As my initial surprise diminished I found myself studying her, she seemed very intent on her water. I tried catching her eye to see if I could work out if she needed anything else but she was obviously avoiding my gaze. It seemed to drift up and then quickly dart away.

Ordinarily I would think she was shy but this felt different. As this silent charade went on for what felt like an age I felt my impatience growing. I was here for her help and we had ended up with her nearly needing first aid before we had even said 'Hello'.

After another minute or so I could feel my face tightening with the unspoken words of the questions that I had. I didn't feel able to ask until she looked like she wasn't going to faint again. I was quite pleased when she finally spoke up

"Okay. You have a lot of talking to do. I know this isn't what you expected. A GP who almost faints when you shake her hand, but that is what you've got and I think that there is something that you have to tell me. To start off we need to go somewhere a bit quieter."

She spoke with quiet authority and despite feeling irritated at how she had kept me waiting her tone of command reassured me a lot.

Although I was still a bit confused and worried about what had just happened. When she told me follow it seemed like the most sensible thing to do in the world, so I did.

As we headed off out the café I felt oddly at peace. The doubts that had been plaguing me were at least temporarily silenced by the mixed-up confidence that I felt in this stranger. It was all based on that feeling of connection. She made me feel safe. Trust has surprised me in the past by cropping up in unexpected locations. I decided that you simply have to go with your instincts sometimes.

Bridget

The next sensation I was aware of was the power surging into my arm as he took my hand. I've not been struck by lightning but if it was anything like this I was certain that I would be burnt to a cinder. Surprisingly it didn't knock me out but for a moment every cell of my being was aligned to this man, the closest equivalent I could imagine was if I was made of iron filings and he was a strong magnet. This was accompanied by the appearance of a second image that overlaid my normal sight.

It was one I was familiar with from various art works, and not an easy one to mistake. It was slightly taller than John but it was very clear. The antlers sprouting from the forehead, accompanied by the greenery that was growing from the face and body, with a wide grin and deep brown eyes that felt they were pulling me in. It was Cernunnos. As the knowledge reached me I heard myself exclaim "Oh my God!" I had never used it more literally than at that moment.

I felt him guide me to a chair and I let it happen while I was trying to catch my breath. The image had gone now, but I was still feeling that the magical overload from that brief contact was buzzing in my blood. I hadn't expected anything like that, but I was now going to have to work it out.

John seemed to be trying to be solicitous for my health, but I needed a bit of space from him so I sent him off with a plea for water. I began to slow my breathing to try and bring the surging energy in my body back under my control.

I had momentarily shelved the questions that were racing in my mind, but as he returned with the glass of water being trailed by a waitress, I still needed some time.

The tingling in my arm had died down to merely irritating pins and needles and I rubbed it to take away the sting. The brief exposure to what seemed to equate to a magical national grid was making me much more cautious. I had to be quite rude and almost snatched the glass from him to prevent any recurring contact in case that made things worse.

The downside of using magic is the increased sensitivity that it generates, the more you use, the stronger your reaction to phenomena like this. I used the water as an excuse to not engage with him properly while allowing myself space to think.

I slowly began to feel I was able to piece things together, and while I had some experience of unusual things this was something new. It was definitely my first encounter with the apparently unwitting avatar of a Celtic deity. The list of people who have shaken hands with a god must be quite small, but it is not as if it was a claim to fame that I would be able to make much use of.

I was still feeling very shaken but letting that surface know would be self indulgence so I needed to work out what was happening.

This meant I need more information, a lot more.

Replaying the momentary vision in my mind I realised that while the mouth was smiling there was a lot of sadness in the eyes. Maybe he was trapped? Was this man somehow acting like a prison cell? I stopped myself, that was just melodramatic claptrap. I had no real evidence for that so I focused on calming myself down further. I needed to regain my professional objectivity and not allow an emotional response to dictate what I needed to do next.

Feeling calmer again, I tried studying John without making eye contact. I was nervous that even that connection would potentially spark something off and I wanted to be more cautious, having been caught out before. I was wary about being pulled in again.

I noted that the maelstrom of energy which had been pulling at me when I entered the café seemed to have died down; it was still there but seemed somehow more muted. It was, I now realised, like being at the eye of the storm. John was somehow generating the disturbance but was immediately buffered from it himself, at least on the physical level. I briefly tried opening up my senses to what was going on and felt the pull of the current tug hungrily at me and I had to shut it down quickly. Another 'no go' for the time being.

From that brief moment I realised something even more worrying. I was not picking up any sense of control. There was a lot of energy out there, but no guiding principle that I was able to discern. A steel cable itself is not that worrying a thing, but there is a huge difference between when it is taut under tension moving a heavy load and watching it flail around wildly.

I carefully edged my awareness closer to John again; while I could tell that he was connected, I wasn't picking up any sort of signals that this was under his control. By opening up I became peripherally aware of his mood. The growing impatience and confusion about what was happening was beginning to spill out of him and I could sense that this was intensifying the energy that was swirling unseen around us.

The atmosphere and attitude of the other patrons seemed to be starting to pick up on this, the mood was turning sour. Tightening of lips, tensing of shoulders, all around us the feedback of this man's mood was beginning to make itself felt. The light coming through the dusty windows dimmed a little. The problem took on yet another layer of complexity and I stepped up my thinking to a faster pace to keep up with the situation as it developed.

I could see that this was going to be a much more entertaining and challenging Friday evening than I had bargained for. I could feel my shock begin to turn to anger, I really disliked surprises, but I realised that was just as unhelpful as my melodrama before, so I focused on being more dispassionate, focusing on the problem at hand. There was a significant magical focus manifest in the body of the man sitting opposite me, who was losing his patience.

I felt his feelings turn towards annoyance and that heated emotion begin to cut through my newly raised defences like an acetylene torch burning through tinfoil. It was time to act, even if I still needed to learn more.

To distract him, and to vent a little of my own emotions, I informed him in one of my most authoritative tones that we had to leave. That seemed to get his attention. We didn't have the luxury of exploring hypothetical scenarios and as the threat was growing I needed to get him away from here. I tried to stand, possibly a little too quickly, but managed to recover myself. John stood up with me, taking the cue that my statement we needed to go was now going to be acted on. He saw me sway and tried to offer his support but I waved it away. Contact was too big a risk at this point, but the automatic concern did endear him to me a bit more. Despite whatever else was happening he seemed to be kind.

To try and secure my authority I risked making eye contact, but wasn't able to hold it long. I was left with the lingering memory of how his eyes were an unusual shade of deep blue. They reminded me of something, but again I realised that this was not the time. I decided to keep it short and instructed him to follow me.

He did so without any argument which was useful. I was still adapting to the results of the magical overload and needed some time to think.

My first, and hopefully best, plan was to get him to the nearest neutral green space. I needed to sit on the grass, near some trees and connect more fully to my own power. Concrete and similar modern products were a slight barrier, but this felt like a big issue so I wanted to be at full capacity. It was possibly also wise to get him away from people if possible, at least in close proximity if the mood of the customers in the café was any sign.

I could feel him behind me, an only slightly reluctant entourage of one. He was both a physical presence and a magical super storm which I felt like I was surfing along the wave front. In combination we seemed to have no trouble with being jostled by pedestrians, our way just opened up before us. Even those ahead of us with their backs turned managed to part before we reached them.

As we approached the traffic lights at the top of Middle Meadow Walk the pedestrian crossing was just turning red. However even though I didn't try and do anything they suddenly flickered and abruptly returned to show us the Green Man to allow us to cross. I quietly muttered "How Apt." It seems that maybe technology does, as some people suspect, have some basic sentience and it wasn't going to get in our way.

I kept a pace or so ahead of him and was scanning the path to gauge how busy the Meadows were going to be. The power flowing around us emanating from John was significant and I wasn't sure how this was going to play out. I was relieved that when we reached the junction where it opened out, I could see that there were not many people sitting around.

The day which had previously been balmy was now feeling distinctly chillier and a gusty wind was pulling at our clothing. The debris of abandoned picnics was visible, it seems the unsettled feeling had encouraged people to leave. Looking up I didn't blame them.

The sky which had been clear blue was now dull with sullen grey clouds stretching from horizon to horizon. It wasn't overcast in the normal sense, but was roiling above us with conflicting movement as if a storm was brewing, but couldn't decide how to break.

I briefly wondered if there was a case of correlation rather than causation when, as John neared the grass, I felt the blast of energy exchange between him and the weather which almost shook me physically.

This was a looking a lot more serious than I had first expected. Small local disturbances in enclosed spaces was one thing, this was starting to look like something else entirely. The scale was enough to give me pause, how far was this going to go. I realised that there was nothing else I could do about it now than give it my best shot.

"Okay. Step 1. Triage." I muttered as we hit the edge of the grass and turned west onto the path which runs along the side of the Old Royal Infirmary. It was currently a building site which was experiencing 'renewal'. The type of work done there was proving to be so radical that I tended to think of it as being another victim of inflicted modernisation.

My tastes were more inclined towards maintaining the old rather than adding modern touches to it. I realised that I was allowing my fear of what was possibly coming next to distract me; I pulled my thoughts back to the problem at hand.

Frantically, trying to come up with the next step in this dance where I couldn't quite hear the tune, I realised that I could feel the tension in my body and could feel it in my throat and noted that anything I said was going to be tinged with that feeling.

The only good thing was that it gave me a feeling of authority that meant there was a better chance that I would be obeyed if I had to give an order. I took a moment and felt my connection to the world deepen. Taking advantage of being out in the urban equivalent of nature.

As I felt the energy surge around me I realised that while I needed this to be stronger, I may have made a fundamental miscalculation. John's symptoms actually seemed to be worsening in this lovely green space. The lack of barriers was reinforcing the problem rather than helping it dissipate as I had initially hoped.

"Sit there!" I pointed at one of the benches that lined the path looking out across the grass. I was suddenly grateful that the Meadows were also more empty at this point of the year. It was possibly fortunate that the odd weather linked to this problem was taking place in the small gap between it being overrun by students and August when it was all festival goers. Crowds would have made this more difficult to keep secret.

I was unable to come up with a better plan at this point, and unwilling to admit to John that I was wrong, so I decided to improvise.

"Feet up!" I ordered somewhat imperiously, but aware that given the way the problem was going I was running out of options. Thankfully John seemed willing to comply with reasonable good grace.

I could tell he wasn't entirely happy, both from his body language and the swirl of emotion that was becoming more obvious to me as I widened my awareness. He settled himself, a little uncomfortably, cross-legged onto the bench.

The irritation I could feel coming off of him in waves was definitely feeding back into the environment. My awareness of magic was screaming like a Geiger counter taken into a faulty nuclear power plant. Having got him settled and contained as best I could in the circumstances, I decided I had to act quickly otherwise there was the chance that the storm would break both metaphorically and literally. That is the problem with magic, metaphor sometimes ceases to apply and thought becomes reality.

Unceremoniously, I sat on the grass, quickly centred myself and adjusted my awareness to the right level. I opened myself to the energy that surrounded us and reached out to try and unravel the current mess. Years of practice, and a natural aptitude had reduced the amount of time that I needed to enter the right state of mind. It is fortunate that I respond well to pressure. Keeping that all-important balance of passion and calm.

Once I was in the correct receptive state I was able to use my mental and magical skills to separate out my awareness.

What people don't appreciate is that there are multiple different levels of reality that we all operate on on a daily basis, but are unaware of; with a bit of practice it is easier to see behind the scenes. I had struggled to try and teach myself some of the principles of theoretical physics which connected to the concept of layers of perception and forms of subjective reality. It hadn't really worked but I could see what they were aiming for. In reality I was able to find a practical application for those ideas, even if the language of the concepts eluded me when kept within their scientific context. It all boils down to the fact that there is more to the world than normal eyes can see.

Given the complexity of the situation I felt it necessary to reduce the distractions that were all too common when you operate on more levels than normal simultaneously. So with a conscious effort I did my best to filter out the empathic awareness of John's anguish, characterised in my mind as a dull throbbing. With that 'eye' shut I was able to focus instead on the level of energy where I could perceive the connections between discrete entities and the world around them. Normally it helped me place myself and manipulate things in my vicinity. However this time my primary goal was to establish exactly what was going on between John and the rest of the world.

As ever my subconscious, like everyone else's, chooses the worst possible moment to interject with suggestions or comments. The current niggle was my growing realisation that I was jumping straight into a magical solution with no idea how I was going to explain it, if it worked, to this man who I hadn't even met properly yet.

Based on our very brief encounter and my assessment of the lack of control I strongly suspected he was going to be fundamentally oblivious to the fact that magic is actually a common element in most people's lives, but which they ignore or misattribute to fortune, or misfortune. I shelved that for the time being, and marked that up as a personal victory for pragmatism and focused instead on my main priority. Reduce the immediate risk to both this man and the world and then work out how much sense it will make to him.

I was deeply aware that symptomatic treatment is never as good as systemic, but given the current situation I was completely out of options.

The surges in the energy around us were obviously strong enough to disrupt weather and I had no idea if there was the potential for other manifestations, and a local weather system was bad enough.

A butterfly can, according to quantum theory, cause a hurricane by flapping its wings. I had no wish to see what was likely to happen with this much energy flying around. I decided that I had to deal with the weather first, before this local disruption went on to have wider consequences. It is normally not easy to control the weather, the variables are many and varied when it is just doing its normal unpredictable thing. The force currently being applied to the strands of energy that made up the weather was immense. I had done a little prodding in the past and then they had always been sluggish to respond to my intent, but under the current influences I felt like I was delving into stone.

I kept my breathing as slow and steady as I could, but I could feel the energy flow through me. My previous attempts had all been minor tweaks to hold off light showers, or align the prevailing conditions to better suit my needs.

This was rare, I had almost never had to go and undo something shaped by another magical will. It was an interesting experience, the quality of intent was very different. It had thankfully not been an active battle of wills, the last time I had been forced into direct conflict with another magic worker had been years previously and it was not an experience I hope to ever have again.

I took several minutes to make sure this was going to work. I alternated between redirecting the flow, draining build-ups and on occasion augmenting some of the sections that felt more 'natural'.

Some of it was pure guesswork, but the energy responded to my efforts and I felt the winds drop and when I opened my eyes I could see the clouds were beginning to break away back into a more normal pattern.

There was still the same magnetic pull about John but I had managed to reduce the intensity at least. The side effect of this I was now buzzing with the after-effect of the power I had been channelling. I felt able to take on the world. It was always the hardest thing about magic, having to stop. It is dangerous to have so much power literally at your fingertips.

Everyone has occasional irrational urges, it is part of being human, where they want to fly either from joy or to get away; or smash things when the anger builds up inside them.

The problem for anyone who is skilled at working with magic is that all of those things are one step closer. An unguarded thought can much more easily become reality. The distinction between whim and action are a bit more blurred unless you have good self-control. That combined with the addictive nature of the flow of power make any significant magical working a dangerous activity. Acknowledging the temptation but controlling it, I focused on gradually releasing the energy back into the world.

It is one of the first things you learn, the importance of grounding the excess energy that is no longer needed back into the earth. This quickly reintegrated itself back into the natural flows I had re-established and left me feeling slightly less inclined towards megalomania.

It would take a little while for my own internal energies to resettle after such a significant exertion, I was still feeling a bit disorientated despite the grounding. Sadly I realised that I still had to deal with the man in front of me. I had only just met him and he had already proven more problematic than my last relationship.

I was uncertain if it was better or worse that he seemed entirely oblivious to what was actually going on. Which meant I needed to find out more. Was he truly unaware that he was causing these problems? I could only do that by asking him some more questions.

"Step 2. Medical History," I stated, engaging him from where I sat on the ground. I didn't trust my feet yet but needing to get things moving again. The mystery of the 'how' and 'why' of this situation were still to be uncovered.

I really hoped he would just tell me what I needed to know. That was looking to be unlikely and I feared it was going to be a long drawn out process of trying to work out what the right questions to ask were. It is often the problem when people don't understand the nature of the issue that they are experiencing, it is the same in medicine as magic, you need more information than 'it hurts'.

"I need you to tell me what it was that made you talk to Maebh. What did you tell her that made her suggest that you talk to me? I know I called it 'medical history' but I don't need to know what immunisations you had.

I need to know what the unusual things that happened were. What is it that you have noticed that is making you feel a bit … worried?"

I made my best attempt at giving him some starting points, but didn't want to lead him too far. I didn't know enough just yet. I had to keep him calm and that was often difficult when the types of solutions that you offered were ones that made most people believe you were crazy.

Being a 'Witch Doctor' made things more interesting, but definitely not easier.
It seems that the relationship between how significant the problems are remains strictly in proportion to how interesting they are: few people for example have difficulty eating doughnuts and while that is enjoyable it is far from a significant act in most situations. I carefully watched his expression, there seemed to be a brief internal struggle but it was short lived and he quickly launched into his explanation.

"Okay, as I said over the phone, I don't want to sound like a loony but for a few days now, lots of weird things have been happening." He was watching my face closely, and I could tell he wasn't yet fully committed to telling me everything so I prompted him as little.

"Weird things?" I could feel my eyebrow raise as I asked this, and quickly brought it back down again. I had to reserve judgement until I knew more. Where on the spectrum of weird were we? For all I knew he thought the moon going away and coming back each month counted as 'weird'. At this point I was presuming he was closer to the mainstream and probably wouldn't know the difference between widdershins and withies.

Everyone has their conceptual threshold, and weird is very subjective.

"Yeah, real weird. Mostly plant related." He paused after saying that, and I think seemed a bit embarrassed by this connection to the chlorophyllic world. "Things started growing really crazily in our flat, like they had all been given a bumper dose of fertiliser, or something."

I could see his discomfort with the topic but decided to leave space for him to carry on, after a moment I resorted to conversational semaphore to indicate he should continue, the head tilt and eyebrow quirk seemed to do the trick.

"Well that was a bit weird, but since it has been such a good summer. I didn't think too much about it, things grow, it happens, all natural." So far so good, but I wasn't hearing anything that made sense as a cause.

As a Doctor a large part of my job was being able to listen to people, and as a Witch that is even more vital, as they may be telling you things without realising it. The evidence was starting to come, but I wasn't clear yet on the cause. I was doing my best not to jump to conclusions as that could be even more dangerous.

The sensation of navigating through conversations about magic with a non-practitioner in trouble was often akin to being on a rollercoaster. The optical illusion of perspective made it look as if the track disappeared, and you kept going but you didn't know it was just a straight drop or one that was going to suddenly veer off to one side. You just hold on the best you can. I nodded encouragingly, allowing him to continue at his own pace.

"So we had this party, for my flatmate's birthday, normal stuff, booze and some special brownies, this was just last weekend, and it was all going fine, bloody plants were everywhere but made it feel sort of tropical.

I was on a bit of a high, not out of it, just had a nice buzz going on and was being silly and didn't notice at first but apparently when I touched any of the plants it started growing really quickly.

Someone else spotted this, can't remember who, but they made me do it more and it was really obvious.

Then for a laugh they put some seeds in my hand and they started sprouting, just there in my hand! I was totally amazed and a bit freaked but it was just so cool, I couldn't stop staring at them. Some people got a bit narky and wanted to know what the trick was, including my girlfriend Susie, that should be my ex-girlfriend."

I nearly winced at the stress he placed on 'ex' as the bitterness in his voice was tangible. I felt my concern growing again, weather was one thing but the ability to force plants into growth, rather than gently coaxing them, was not an easy one. Seeds were even more tricky – the factors that needed to be manipulated and balanced were complex.

The fact that he had been doing so without there being any conscious direction was both impressive and worrying. I was starting to move towards a conclusion but didn't want to pre-empt it in case there was something more to be said that would change the situation.

"Anyway, everyone was a bit drunk by this stage, people started getting in my face about the seeds and the plants wanting to know how I did it, and if it was a wind up.

Susie started shouting at me about keeping secrets and other crap that I apparently did that pissed her off, but she had been storing it all up and decided that this was the best possible moment to have a go at me about them."

I could feel John's sadness at the memory of the argument, and the betrayal he felt at being made a target for something he didn't understand or control. It spilled out from him in a cold wave, letting me know that my empathy had come back online after my recent attempt to filter it out. I couldn't help the expression of sympathy that my face adopted, it was just too raw a feeling. It was also informed by my own experience. I managed to only think 'Ah, one of those' rather than say it, as it would be too pointed. I had never understood those people who stored up grievances in a relationship rather than air them quickly. It stopped people from either moving on from something dysfunctional or allowing you to resolve the problem and move on to the making up which could be so much more fun.

John carried on with his tale, I could see the relief that he experienced just from being able to talk as a visible lessening of tension in his shoulders and posture. I sat watching him closely, he realised that he had paused in the narrative to wallow in the injustice of wounded feelings.

Catching himself in the silence he quickly looked up to ensure that he still had my attention. He obviously appreciated my expression was one of sympathy as I got a small nod from him and after another moment he returned to his story.

"So, since I was also confused and a bit scared by it all, I just couldn't help myself. I started shouting back and getting sort of heated. People had started leaving once Susie got in my face about things, my flatmate had basically run away to his bedroom to avoid all the shit that was going down.

Anyway as I started shouting all of the plants started going crazy some of them getting really big and some of them dying, and anything with a seed in it started growing.

Susie just freaked out totally at that point and ran out of the flat. To be honest, I know it sounds bad but, I was really glad to see the back of her, she had basically said it was over and that I was a liar so all that was left was a flaming row. I was left there on my own and had no idea what to do so I sat and drank the rest of the booze that I could find."

Having covered this dramatic finale I watched as he slumped just a little bit more into the bench.

The last tension disappearing, it is always cathartic to be able to speak honestly with someone, even if they are a stranger. However I wasn't able to relax, this wasn't a sharing session, I now had to act.

Having now heard his story I was impressed, and worried. He was going through a fairly sustained, potentially traumatic, and obviously magical experience but hadn't completely lost his mind.

The risks of uncontrolled magic were significantly worse than that of controlled magic. Insanity as a consequence of intensive use of magic was a fairly common problem even for skilled magic users. So when you factor in that he apparently had no training I was impressed with his resilience in the face of a serious problem.

Sadly I feared that we weren't yet out of trouble and I hoped he had some left, otherwise he may end up cracking under the pressure. The manifestations were very strong, and I was still not yet at the heart of the issue.

"I woke the next day expecting to feel really rough" John continued, he was much more relaxed now and it came more easily, "but oddly I didn't – not a hangover, nothing. Felt as fresh as the proverbial daisy." The disbelief that he obviously felt at the miraculous avoidance of what should have been a most epic hangover still remained with him.

"I found a note from my flatmate saying he was off to visit his folks for a week or so. Not too odd as he disappears off all the time, but I strongly suspect this time was due to the fact it all got weird and he was more than a little freaked by it all and just wanted to put as much distance between him and me as possible."

I sat watching him wondering what was next, as the story was apparently far from over. Even in isolation the incident he described from the party would have been a good basis for seeking out some advice, either supernatural or psychiatric.

"So I cleared up the flat, all the fallen leaves and stuff like that and it had settled down again, no massive reactions by the plants or anything."

John blushed a little as he confided the next bit. "I even tried to make some stuff happen, you know, repeat the seeds thing or make the plants react, but nothing happened, so I sort of felt I could laugh it all off as a one-off really weird party and move on."

I suppressed a smile, I recall the early days of when I learnt magic, and trying things out. This made it clear that he didn't know what had caused it so hadn't been able to tap into the right mindset. I could see however that while he was reliving the relief that he had felt, it was tinged with the memory of what had come after this, that apparently couldn't be as easily laughed off.

"A couple of days after the party there was a sneaky little BBQ up on Calton Hill, just a few friends and a few beers, not too heavy for a midweek night.

The weather was just so gorgeous and you get great views up there. So I went along and was having a great time, was able to feel normal. And no one mentioned the party so it was even better.

As the evening wore on, it was so nice and warm just sitting in the sun, surrounded by friends all having a laugh. I just nodded off. When I did though I had the weirdest dream, nothing really clear, nothing concrete, but it was very ... well sexual.

It felt like I was floating in a really warm sea, all I remember was the warmth, and I was surrounded by strange lights and colours and, well, a lot of... sensations."

I noticed that he blushed slightly as he got onto this topic, he seemed to take a quick glance at me and then away, I could feel his discomfort, but there was an added layer that even talking about the memory was bringing back some of the same sensations.

I put in place an additional barrier to my empathy as his feelings were echoing with me a little too much. He was a nice looking man, but I had to sustain my professionalism. He was a patient in need and I have my ethics, so I couldn't think of him as a man at the moment. As tempting as I found it.

"I don't know why but I woke up suddenly, and well, it was to find that everyone around me was getting it on in some way, not quite an orgy, but definitely more than just friends sitting around having a laugh. I was a bit freaked out actually and decided to get out of there, but what was even weirder was that as I tried to get away I tripped over some bushes that were just where my head had been, and they definitely hadn't been there when I had lain down."

In the pause that followed this additional revelation I wasn't able to stop myself from blurting out "So then what happened?" This obviously startled him out of his reverie, but seemed to put him into a more matter of fact mode, although his calm was still under strain.

"I ran off home as fast as I could. It was all a bit much, it was all too weird and I seemed to be at the heart of it each time. So I went into hiding. Went home to bed and tried to get some sleep but I ended up having a bit of a weird dream.

And this morning I found a shit load of moss in my bedroom. I was on the verge of going to a hospital to get myself committed. If Maebh hadn't shown up at the flat offering to help, that is where I would be now. I assume someone at the BBQ had noticed something and told her I had run off, or something?"

The last 'or something' was mumbled as he lapsed back into a mood of withdrawn concern. The power of doubt had taken hold of him again, the subtext was clear. He was thinking he should have gone to the hospital. It was as if he had heard his own story properly himself for the first time when he spoke it out loud.

I could feel the confidence ebbing out of him, his opinion of himself seemed to have swung entirely towards 'psychotic episode'; rather than 'mystical event'.

"Interesting." I decided to let that sum it all up. It was best to keep things basic, and I felt foolish after my previous excited outburst. Now I was certain he had finished I began turning it all over in my mind. Was there anything in what he had said that worked against my first presumption?

The vision of the Horned God had definitely thrown me, but I wasn't hearing a cause. Just a lot of consequences and effects.

He hadn't made any reference to things which would show he was aware of this connection. So the symptoms of his problem were clear, and I had a theory but I was reluctant to just presume that I was right, even though it was tempting. I looked up at him.

"Do you really believe me?" his expression of fearful hope was enough to confirm that I would do what I could to help. It was a central tenet of my personal code, if someone in genuine need asks you for something that you can do, never refuse them lightly. So even if this situation had merely been disentangling a small piece of apparently magically crossed wires causing the occasional burst of mood inspired growth in place of fertiliser I would have considered helping out.

His distress was genuine and that spoke to my compassion, which was reinforced by my oath as a Doctor. I knew very well the genuine psychological harm that protracted magic can cause, even in the best of circumstances. This situation was obviously far from the best.

Regardless of my human feelings and my medical training the situation was one that called to me as a Witch. He was displaying a strength of power that had me slightly in awe, the local disruption to the weather patterns was no simple thing especially as he was not even aware of what was happening. This could have a massive ecological impact if I didn't intervene, as magic can often make things cascade further if not properly limited. So all of the factors combined to make me commit to helping him. All that remained now was for me to work out what was going on beneath the surface.

John

I realised I had sort of zoned out while telling Bridget what had happened to me. It felt so weird actually saying it all out loud. When you put it all together like that in one conversation it felt truly bizarre and I had no idea what she was going to make of it all. She was definitely a bit weird herself, but I found it kind of reassuring. It took weird to deal with weird. She had been really bossy, no commanding, it made me feel like she was in charge. That was despite the fact that she'd fainted when we first met.

If we had met under other circumstances I would have tried to flirt with her more. She was attractive in a severe sort of way. I could feel that she was kind but it wasn't the normal soft kindness. It was strong. I normally go with my first impressions and today had been something special. From the static spark to the immediate feeling of connection, it made me doubt that this was the first time we had met. I felt a bit calmer and was able to breath a bit more easily. I realised that what I really wanted was for it all to go away. I just wanted the world to make sense again.

I ran out of words. So I stopped talking, wondering how she would respond. I was half expecting her to freak out, but she actually seemed to believe me. She just said "Interesting". It was a lot better than I had hoped, I thought she would have just run off. At best a shouted "goodbye" as she ran away.

She seemed to be handling it really well, better than I had. Maybe that meditating she had done when we arrived had mellowed her out.

I'd not tried it before properly, but maybe meditating was more than just sitting quietly for a bit. I still didn't entirely believe that she wasn't kidding. I searched her face looking for any sign that it was a wind up. I had to ask if she seriously believed me.

She gave me a small nod, that was all. I became aware I had been holding myself tense, the muscles in my back and neck relaxed. Just having that acknowledgement was enough. Her next words shocked me, I really wasn't expecting her to say "But how did this happen?"

It was basically muttered but was such a clear throw away comment. It meant that she actually knew what was happening. My heart jumped in my chest. She knew. Somehow she knew what was happening. She could help.

"What? How did what happen?" I leapt up, not able to stop myself. The adrenaline flooding my system felt good. I nearly trod on her, managing to just miss her. This was great. Now we were getting somewhere. I felt so happy!

She stumbled to her feet after I had found my footing and she stood there holding her hands out, as if she was blocking me. I didn't expect her to go back to ordering me around. But she almost shouted "Sit down for god's sake!" She pointed at the bench. She was clearly startled by something and her eyes kept darting to my feet. It was only then that I looked down.

Around my feet the grass had grown a few inches in a circle from where I was standing, spreading out for a few feet. There were even some small flowers peeking out from between my shoes.

The ground had been bare earth when we sat down. The grass worn to mud by the feet of the people using the bench. The clouds broke overheard and a beam of sunshine shone down on us.

I was shocked by this new sign of weirdness but this time it didn't completely knock me down. I was getting some answers and that gave me hope. I reluctantly sat down again, realising that this was serious, but I felt so much more in control. Bridget seemed to be able to understand and was willing to help so I wanted to keep her on side. So I decided not to try and agree, in case that pissed her off, but she wasn't getting out of my sight until she had helped fix this. Whatever 'this' was. I needed answers, and she seemed to be able to give them to me.

"Fine, I'm sitting. Now it is your turn to talk. What's happening to me?" I tried to make eye contact with her again, but she seemed to be avoiding looking directly into my eyes.

She was obviously struggling with something internally, but I wasn't entirely sure what. It reminded me of some of the awkward flirting that I had done as a teenager, but there was obviously more than that going on here. Neither of us were teenagers anymore and she had shown her confidence and strength of will before, so something wasn't right.

Whatever was upsetting her passed very quickly. It was only a second or so, but I was watching her so closely it was easy to get some clues. Once she was back in control of herself it was like a wall had gone up.

The only thing I could tell was that she was running words through her mind before speaking. I kept on watching her really closely. It was interesting to see when she finally seemed to settle on how she wanted to phrase whatever it was she was going to tell me.

"Have you heard of the condition known as SAD, S.A.D.?"

She sounded tentative, like she wasn't sure I would be able to follow her. I had a few friends who had sunlamps they used over winter so it was something I had a clue about. I nodded.

"Seasonal Affective Disorder. Right? But doesn't that only work in the winter? You know, it's winter and too dark and that makes people depressed and all that stuff." I really didn't see what the connection was between me and what she was saying.

She nodded and I could see a flicker of relief that I was with her so far, that obviously made the next things she wanted to say easier

"Well, yes. That is normally the case, and it is clear that you get the idea. This is obviously more complicated as what we have here is what I would refer to as a bad case of Reciprocal Seasonal Affective Disorder."

She had switched her tone, and now it sounded much more like when I had been at the Doctors and been given a diagnosis before, calm but very clear. It was reassuring to hear it put in simple terms, but I still didn't quite get it.

"Reciprocal? Are you saying that my mood affects the weather as well as the other way around?"

The concept was truly bizarre, but seemed to fit what had happened. It just didn't sound possible. I struggled with the idea. It sort of felt right, but sounded unreasonable.

"Basically, yes. It is a bit more than that, but that will serve for now." Bridget seemed much more assertive again and seemed to be willing to meet my gaze, but I could tell she was still uncomfortable. There was this odd pulling sensation when I looked into her eyes and while I enjoyed being able to look at her, I decided to look away.

"Oh, okay. But how?" I looked down at the taller grass and flowers that had appeared recently. It was much harder for me to refuse that this was true when I could see what I had apparently done. Even if I didn't know how.

"You are apparently attuned to the energies that underpin the natural world to an unusual degree, and somehow that is allowing you to influence things around you. But only when you are in the right emotional state. So far it seems to be limited to only the immediately surrounding area. I think you might be doing some sort of channelling."

I listened to what she was saying but the ideas she was trying to get across to me just sounded like the worst hippy claptrap. When she got to 'channelling' it was just too much to bear. Was she going to hold a séance? Did she think I was actually getting involved with ghosts?

"Well.. " I started to interject. To bring it back to a sane context.

"No! Listen to me a bit longer. Did you just want me to tell you that this was all a mistake and it would just disappear on its own? Or that here was a handy little pill and that is you sorted?

Some sort of personal magic weed killer? I am not going to let you dismiss this so lightly. Use your eyes! Think about what has been happening here, what you have seen, what you have felt. I know that it might be easier to just say it is all impossible."

I looked up at her, she was standing in front of me, using her hands to illustrate her points as she made them. The obvious anger that she felt at what I was about to say, and somehow she had known what that was going to be, even before I said it. I was a bit stunned, but was very impressed by the force of what she was saying.

"Okay, I understand it is difficult for you. Our society has moved to the point where science is all, and magic is a nice set of lies for children. A simple fairytale. But that isn't the whole truth. If you even ask some scientists they will tell you we don't have all the answers, there is a lot more to the world than most people see."

As she continued, I was feeling like an insect on her windscreen as she powered on with her reasoning. Her voice pitched a little lower and her body language shifted to now be more open. I could tell she was now obviously trying to appeal to the fact that I clearly didn't have all the answers and there was more to what she was saying than I was automatically ready to hear.

"Do you want me to try and explain this as a type of quantum phenomena? Do you want to hear how reality as we perceive it is just a construct that does not reflect the true nature of what surrounds us?

I can try and make it sound much more technical. However what it all boils down to is that your problem falls into the area that current science regards as magical, and until such time as they get around to studying all this, you will have to deal with the fact that I am, as a Witch, your only hope for getting this resolved. If you want to go on as you are, and try and get yourself committed to a mental institution go ahead. I'm sure they will find you very handy in the gardens."

I watched her, she was now studying me intently. The additional stuff she had said, the way she had stopped me from just making a joke out of it made me stop and think. I had seen a lot of stuff, her argument that it was a bit of weird science that only made sense on the quantum level gave me some reassurance.

I still wasn't entirely sure on how to proceed. I actually felt a bit embarrassed that I had nearly been so quick to dismiss what she was offering to do for me.

"I just sort of hoped... Maebh seemed to imply..." I tried to start a few times, but really couldn't find the right words to explain how I had felt, and how I was now feeling. Bridget's expression had suddenly become a lot more thoughtful, she had been struck by something I had said. She was now studying my face in detail, as if she was memorising it. I was a bit startled when she suddenly shouted at me.

"Maebh! How do you know Maebh?"

This change in direction confused me, she had gone from talking about my symptoms and science and was now asking about my social life and how I was referred on to her. I just couldn't follow it, she didn't make any sense to me.

"I know her through Beltane. I thought that was how you knew her too?"

I was watching her face closely and when I said Beltane I could see something in her face, she wasn't surprised, it was if she had known already that was going to be the answer.

"No. I don't know her through Beltane, we... let's just say that we know each other of old. I know what you mean by Beltane though, and I think that this may help me pinpoint the source of the problem. Tell me, what part did you play in the most recent one?"

I was still a bit confused by the change in direction, but I could tell from the tension in her face, and the way her voice had gone very calm and level that there was something else going on.

"Oh, I was the Green Man. I had to wear this sort of monstrous walking hedge costume. Have you seen it before? It was so exciting to be part of such a big festival. It went so quickly, you would think that as it takes hours to walk around in a big procession it would be a nightmare but it was so quick! Each elemental point just came and went in a bit of a blur.

Once we got to the stage bit, the Green Man, that was me, had to walk around and then touch the May Queen. That was when they pretended to kill me, her handmaidens that was, the "Whites" just a group of people painted white to represent purity, nothing racist. They are the opposite force to the 'Reds' who are about chaos and lust.

Anyway, after I get 'killed' the May Queen then brings me back to life. It was such a trip, acting out the whole death and rebirth journey.

I then ended up dancing around almost naked in front of thousands of people. It is all about showing how vital and happy I am that new life is coming to the world."

I realised I had chatted on for what felt like ages, but it was such a relief to be able to talk about something that felt normal. I looked up and Bridget however was sitting there, smiling and nodding. Looking much more relaxed than she had before, it made me feel better and I risked smiling at her a little.

"And what is the Green Man?" Bridget asked me, seeming to be weighing me up in some way that I couldn't quite place.

It was like she was interested in me, but there was something else in it that made me a little uncomfortable.

"Oh, yeah. Well, the Green Man. He's sort of nature, an expression of fertility, and the green energy is all about growth..."

As the words came out of my mouth I could feel the bits of my mind suddenly just clicking together. I felt so stupid. How had I not been able to see that there was a connection?

"But that was just... I wasn't told... I never..." I suddenly felt cold. My legs began to shake. I sat down on the bench again. I couldn't work out what was happening. It just didn't make any sense. I couldn't help myself, the tears just welled up inside and I started sobbing.

I could hear Bridget making some comments but I couldn't really pick up what it was, it felt like my head was stuffed with wool. As I sat there, I felt a growing sense of isolation, a disconnection between myself and my body.

I barely registered when Bridget patted me on my shoulder, it was like it was happening through very thick padding. I started to see the pattern more clearly, the plants, the weird dreams, it all linked back to Beltane. I felt as if I was unravelling and I couldn't work out what was real anymore. I just sank deeper into the feeling and let it all go. It felt weirdly peaceful.

"Stop that!" Bridget shouted at me. I snapped back into focus. She was leaning down into my face, barely inches away and I was shocked to see her in so close. I could see her eyes clearly. She seemed to be really angry at me.

It dawned on me she was doing her best to snap me out of the funk I was slipping into. She continued, now she could see I was paying attention again.

"You have responsibilities. At least until we get this sorted. You can't just sit there and wallow. It will just spread out from you and affect the world. Look around! I will do what I can to help you but you have to do what I say!"

As I looked around I realised that the clouds had come back in again, and the wind was cold. As I pulled myself together I felt the wind drop.

The rain also stopped.

It suddenly felt far too quiet. I could feel my heart beating inside me, the atmosphere felt like there was going to be a storm any second. It might be good if it did, to break the tension in the air.

I looked at her, this stranger who was agreeing to help me. I took the stillness and turned it into calm. A slow deep breath later I looked at her and accepted that this was what we needed to do.

"Do what you can." I said, feeling both optimistic that this would work, but also quite detached from the whole situation.

I suddenly felt embarrassed by it all again. So I looked down. Breaking eye contact and just waiting to see what would happen next. I could see Bridget sit on the ground in front of me again. Letting out another deep breath I let myself relax further.

I watched her for a short while, she seemed to be meditating again. I wondered if she was going to try and teach me how to do that. The previous attempts had mostly resulted in me falling asleep. I guess that if you are trying to reach a different state of consciousness through meditation, unconsciousness doesn't really count as a controlled change.

"Step Three was diagnosis, we did that, so now Step Four. Treatment." Bridget seemed distracted again, she even held up a finger to ask for a moment. What would she do next?

Bridget

It didn't know how simple this would be. He seemed confused when I asked him how he knew Maebh. The shape of my suspicion for the cause was getting there, and was confirmed when he said 'Beltane'. All I had to do was help him join the dots and see how long it took him to make the connection.

He had thankfully opened his mind enough to my earlier challenge so that when I was able to get him to actually think about the situation. It was perfect but he wasn't fighting me quite as much as he would have otherwise. I let him go on about the symbolism, I knew that already.

It was interesting to see how he was able to reflect on it. Obviously there were still some serious pagans involved who would have helped him fill in the background.

He was a handsome man, so there was a chance that his main logic for being involved in that role was closer to the fact he wasn't body conscious and felt able to represent fertility.

I realised that I must have seen photos of him in body paint, Maebh was keen on taking me through the events. I suppressed the inappropriate urge to quip that I hadn't recognised him with his clothes on. He was obviously upset and this didn't feel like the right moment for flirtatious ice breaking.

On one level I was actually enjoying listening to him talk, it was giving me more of an insight into his personality.

He was enthusiastic, seemed reasonably coherent, but was still not demonstrating that he had any real awareness of the esoteric side of the festivals. All he said so far showed that he was able to retain some of the basic context and symbolism.

I could tell when it all slotted into place. The evident shock that transformed his face was sufficient to show that he had worked it out. Given how he had been talking about the event, the moment he put it together was obviously quite traumatic for him. It was so far beyond his normal frame of reference, I hoped that he was strong enough to cope with the reality.

If he had only thought about it as a performance role it was probably akin to an actor suddenly being possessed by the spirit of Hamlet and pining to return to Elsinore. This is not an easy thing to reconcile. I watched him closely for signs that things might be about to get worse. I could have accidentally induced another moment of crisis.

He went very withdrawn so I tried to bring him out of himself again, not quite sure how to help but trying to reach him while he struggled with the turmoil. It got quite bad. The emotional impact of the truth was nearly overwhelming. I could feel a torrent of energy spill out from him. A hundred tendrils of powerful and conflicting emotion reached out and fed his feelings into the surrounding environment. The wind picked up and the clouds gathered. A fine rain began to fall on us.

Through my other senses I could feel a more deeply unsettling stirring in the ground beneath me as the earth began to respond more sluggishly to the changing emotions. Around us the flowers, grass and trees all seemed to be struggling between growth and decay. It was a frenzied conflict at a cellular level that gave them strange strobing auras. I had to stop this. I only had one tactic left. Shock. So I shouted at him, breathing a sigh of relief when it seemed to work.

He pulled himself together, and that is exactly how it felt in the energy around us. The torrent of energy stopped for a breath and then it reversed. A sudden switch from blow to suck. John was there with me, no longer lost in his own feelings. He felt focused. I explained the situation to him. It was clear to me that until we got this under control his behaviour was going to be dangerous if he let his mood rule things.

I felt it necessary to reassure him, and following my natural urge I put a hand on his shoulder. The fabric numbed the impact but there was still a minor jolt of power. I felt it cascade up my arm and pass through my head. As I looked at John he was briefly superimposed with an image of a shadowy set of stubby antlers and traces of ivy in his hair and around his face. I was grateful that it was only temporary and that I hadn't touched his skin again, fainting again would not have been a good idea. It is unfortunate that there isn't a government health warning available along the lines of 'perceiving magical realms can seriously distort your depth perception'. I still swayed a little and wasn't quite able to focus properly for a few seconds.

"I'll do what I can to help you." I wasn't clear which of the images I was actually making my promise to, the fear I had that this was a possession was growing. The atmosphere was still, but heavy, similar in intensity to how it felt before a storm. I suddenly became concerned I had gone too far. The power that he now seemingly had under control could just as easily be unleashed again against me. The dual man/god who was in front of me might try his hand at an experimental smiting, not something that I wanted to experience.

"Do what you can." I was relieved by the content of the message, but the voice to my ears was also now resonating with the aural equivalent of the double vision I had seen and that was far more disconcerting. The harmony of two voices pitched slightly apart but speaking as one penetrated into my mind. It didn't feel so much as permission for me to act but more like a prophecy or a simple statement of incontrovertible fact. I now had to make good on my word. It didn't feel like a choice anymore. The only problem was, I still hadn't the faintest clue what I was actually going to do to fix it.

I thought about what I knew. I had seen an avatar of a nature god and there was a lot of energy flowing from this seemingly oblivious man. The checklist reminded me I was still buzzing with the latest overload, and visualised the problem, turning my awareness back to the level where I could perceive the power and began to direct it back into the local environment.

Carefully balancing the reintegration and allowing my own body to come back to a normal level of energy.

As I felt it flow, and I returned to a calm centre, it came to me: this might be the very key to the problem. John was completely unaware of the energy that he was casually manipulating.

He had demonstrated that he wasn't familiar with the concepts behind it, as he had been resistant to even the idea of magic. So despite his involvement, he wasn't a believer in that side of things. Magic and energy were just words to him, not elements of his life.

From what I recall Maebh saying about Beltane he was probably told about energies, but for a lot of people it remains very figurative, or symbolic of something psychological.

In this case it was actually terrifyingly literal, there was a genuine force to be reckoned with. What I had to do was work out how to help him rebalance things. To do that I would have to get to the heart of what had triggered this off. Beltane had been happening for years and so far none of the other Green Men seem to have ended up in this state, so there was something else at play. I had to work out what.

I had to be careful, his obvious lack of awareness meant that he had no control. The consequences of his emotions were all too apparent. It would all reinforce the damage. I was going to have to get quite psychological to unpick this issue, and for that I needed him to trust me. The level of power he was wielding was immense and could not only harm him, but could cause serious damage to the wider world.

Also how reciprocal was the connection, when you got right down to it? The weather was just the start of it; if he went unchecked it might reach beyond a local effect and spread gods' knows where. The power was able to manifest in different ways, so it could eventually do anything. He was apparently currently sane, which was a blessing, but if he lost his mind which was possible, he would become extremely dangerous. I decided that I needed to get to know him better and then take some steps to fix this.

I had to take charge and see what I could do.

"Step Three was diagnosis, we did that, so now Step Four. Treatment." I did my best to sound positive and confident, which was only partly a lie. I felt I could do this, I just had to work out what and take some time before acting, as this was not a situation where I felt it would be good if I slipped up.

"So what do we do? What do I do?" John asked. I could tell he was continuing in the poised and powerful calm which had fallen around us after my shock tactics. It might have worked, it certainly had resolved the immediate crisis, but we were possibly just on a small plateau of shock, which could crumble at any point. The energy around us was echoing the subdued mood, even the sunlight seemed to be a little dimmer. I scanned the area around us, but there were no outward signs of anything worthy of comment. Normality seemed to be returning. I held up a finger to indicate that I would be with him shortly, my split focus was taxing my attention after I had been so badly rattled by the recent surges in power.

"Well…" I began but was rudely interrupted by a particularly large and cold raindrop choosing that moment to drip from the tree above us and fall onto my neck. I couldn't help what came out of my mouth next. It amused John I could tell, but was not the sort of language I normally used when I first met someone.

My train of thought was completely derailed, but it also seemed to break the tension. John was mostly failing to keep a straight face, his eyes were twinkling with suppressed laughter. I realised how ridiculous it all was and also had a brief struggle not to laugh out loud as well.

"Well, right, now. Dinner. I'm starving. It's been a long day and we have a lot to do later." I decided to get things back on track and used my most matter of fact voice. This afternoon was proving to be one of extreme transitions and was more than a little ridiculous, but you have to go with it. I strongly suspected this would not be the last of it, so we might as well have a meal while I worked it out. John briefly laughed at the sudden change and his expression relaxed into an easy smile.

"We are going to find some food. Both of us need grounding and food is the perfect way to do that." As John stood up I almost went to take his arm. An unconscious act part inspired by the sense of connection that I was already feeling for this stranger, partly by the possessive urge that came from him being my patient and perhaps partly by some feelings of attraction towards him and the power he was manifesting.

I quickly suppressed that as being massively unprofessional. Also the risk of another surge at this point was still strong, so I masked the potentially awkward moment by turning the movement into a mildly theatrical bow, and indicating the direction I felt we should head in.

"After you my good sir!" I said as we started back towards the centre of town. Feeling excited and keen to see where this would lead me.

John

Bridget looked so serious, she seemed to be listening intently but I couldn't hear what would be keeping her attention. She seemed to be back with me when I saw the blur of a giant raindrop fall between us and enter at the neck of her shirt. She started swearing, quite an impressive flow to be honest and it was such a contrast to how composed she had been before that it was hilarious.

Her expression seemed a bit dangerous so I stopped myself from laughing out loud. Thankfully it didn't last long and we exchanged a quick look when she composed herself, it made me feel more relaxed. Once she calmed down she suggested that we go for dinner. I realised that I was also utterly starving, I nodded my agreement and quickly stood up.

She made an odd sort of bow and pointed back towards the centre of town. It felt good to just be walking along with her. We managed to find things to talk about that were apart from what we had just been experiencing, that had all been so intense it was nice to just have a relaxed conversation.

Unfortunately I realised that we couldn't talk about the weather, as a normal ice breaker, and she didn't bring it up either so we managed somehow to avoid that normal British default. We talked about food options and preferences, which were not limited at all, and no odd dietary complications so our options remained open.

We agreed on one of the nearby restaurants and headed back the way we had come. We were lucky that we were able to get a table despite the fact it was a Friday night as we were still quite early for dinner.

A couple of times while we waited for our food I tried to find out what she was thinking about my situation, but she was very skillful at avoiding my questions. We chatted about all sorts of things and it all felt so very natural. I felt nice and relaxed with her and it was just really fun to have an interesting conversation.

Bridget seemed occasionally surprised by some of the snippets I was able to drop in on different topics, and that made me feel more confident. I liked feeling knowledgeable and had a store of random facts in my head that I just seemed to pick up here and there. I really wanted to make a good impression on her, not only as I was feeling a bit awkward over my need for help, but also as I found her attractive.

As we relaxed a bit more, I found myself just enjoying her company. Part of my mind started thinking of this as a really bizarre blind date situation, although I couldn't shake the thought that kept popping back up that this was still very weird. I decided to try and flirt a little and see what happened. If she responded that was good, if not, that was also fine, just meant I had to realise she didn't feel the same.

I still slipped up a bit and couldn't stop myself from bringing up something connected to my 'problem'. She kept us off that topic, but I noticed that she was gradually responding more to my minor flirtatious efforts.

By the time we reached dessert we were chatting like we had known each other for ages and I was almost able to forget why we were here.

When they brought coffee I felt her position shift a bit. She started asking me about Beltane.

It felt a bit more formal but reminded me why we were here and that I needed her help. It was still a good chat but I felt that the focus of her attention was more analytical again. I was being studied. I did my best to tell her what I knew about Beltane, and the other festivals, and there were some questions that she asked that I just had to shake my head and indicate that I really had no idea what she was asking me.

I could see her brows tighten when that happened, as if she was mentally recalculating her opinion of me. Doing my best to just go with it and not worry that I was giving the 'wrong' answers and just be honest.

When they brought the bill we had a brief disagreement over who was paying, but we eventually decided just to split it evenly. As they took away the small plastic tray with the tip Bridget made eye contact with me to share her plan.

"So, now we are a bit more grounded and I know you a bit better, this is what is going to happen. We are going to leave here and head back to mine where I am going to see if I can help you get this 'mix-up' sorted out." I could tell from her tone that she was trying to be serious but not make it sound life threatening.

I wondered what she would have said if I had turned around and said "Nah, not tonight." I wanted this sorted so I didn't have any real choice.

So I nodded and we left the table. I managed to hold the door for her, which earned me a nod of gratitude that made me feel a bit happier. I could still do simple things like that, holding up my side of normality as much as possible.

"Okay, that is fine by me." I decided to try and get the conversation moving again as we went down the street "But you haven't really explained what's happened to me." This seemed to upset her as she turned abruptly and glared at me. I carried on quickly.

"Don't get me wrong. You've made it clear that this is because I was the Green Man back at Beltane. That I have some sort of 'natural' connection that isn't working properly. But I really don't get the 'How it happened', or to sound pathetic briefly 'Why me?'" I hoped that being honest with her would help. I really was lost. It just didn't make sense. I think despite my best efforts to keep it jokey that final 'why me' had actually been quite pathetic, but it had happened and I needed her help. Watching her closely she was obviously considering what to say next. I breathed a little sigh of relief when I saw the tension go out of her shoulders before she spoke. Whatever it was she was about to say was not going to be a fight.

"Fine" she sighed at me. I could tell there was something more coming but didn't know what it was going to be. I decided to keep my mouth shut and go with it, rather than risk upsetting her again.

"There are certain natural forces that exist, and the Celts, amongst others, tried to understand and to a certain extent worshipped. This is clear from the little that most people understand of the old religions. They did this by living in harmony with the natural patterns they observed in the world and in themselves.

A fundamental part of the pattern is the duality of everything: male/female; summer/winter; life/death; light/dark.

All living things have this balance and the state of everything is cyclical. What you did, for the purpose of the Beltane ritual, was to personify the rebirth of the summer male energy from the death of the winter male energy – the 'walking hedge' as you termed it. For most people that is as far as it goes. The energy exists and the ritual acknowledges this, and helps people connect to the cycle to maintain their own harmony."

She looked over at me, gauging my reaction. It actually made sense. It sounded a lot like what some of the other hippies had said when they explained the festival to me, but I had always thought of it as a vague theoretical thing, a bit of cultural history. This was instead an actual thing. That had to be dealt with. I nodded, feeling that this was starting to help me see how this could be happening.

"What I suspect is that you were somehow unusually susceptible to the energy that you were representing, for whatever reason.

You are a pretty unique individual as I think we would have noticed if this had happened to every Green Man, as there have been quite a few of them over the years.

What I further suspect and this is just my theory at this point is this. That possibly due to your lack of awareness or connection to the bigger cycles, the 'force' of the Green Man hit a blockage and is building up inside you behind something like a psychic dam.

After several weeks this build up of energy is now beginning to spill over into the surrounding world to let off the pressure that has built up."

Again she looked at me, I was nodding along. It felt so weird to be discussing these things while walking through the Grassmarket. The pubs and shops were just so normal and here this woman was explaining to me that I was bunged up with some weird energy that was spilling out; the weirdest bit was, it made sense.

"Does this sound plausible?" She was obviously looking for me to actually respond. It wasn't just a rhetorical question. I weighed up everything she had said, while it was alien to me it actually seemed to sound right.

I had hoped that by seeing this doctor that she would give me a way out of the insanity that seemed to be happening, and instead I was being offered what might be a different, but much more attractively packaged form of insanity.

The Celtic backdrop helped it make sense. I wasn't just a fruitcake who was cracking up, there was a genuine problem that I just didn't understand. Since the alternative was accepting that I was most likely going to end up in long term psychiatric care, and that wasn't entirely off the table yet, this option was much nicer.

She was very persuasive, the matter of fact way in which she set it out helped. She was very reassuring and I was aware that I was finding her more attractive as I spent more time with her. I don't know which of these was at the top of my mind but I wanted to trust her.

"Aren't you supposed to say 'Trust me I'm a Doctor' or something when telling people stuff they don't want to believe?" I asked trying to see if I could make her smile.

I had enjoyed a few brief glimpses of it over dinner when relaxed a little more, it was a lovely smile. She smiled.

I smiled in return chalking that up as a personal victory for not being completely out of control, if I could still make jokes that worked.

"I've known too many doctors to ever use that phrase with confidence." She responded obviously amused at my cheekiness.

"Come on." We resumed our walk to her home. "So, do you agree so far? I am aware this is the quick sketch version of things, but I can't actually help you if you aren't with me at least a little bit." She was obviously still testing me in someway, but it felt much less confrontational than before.

"No, yes, sorry, I do." I stammered, my mouth not quite in line with my brain for a moment, "It is all just so new and completely off my normal radar that I'm having to run to keep up with it all." I tried to smile at her to show that everything was fine. I noticed that she was still avoided keeping eye contact with me, which I was still trying to work out. Nothing else indicated that she was a shy person. She sighed, but it sounded like she was relieved, rather than further frustrated by me.

We carried on walking in silence for a bit. I fell back to thinking about what she had said, how the world I had dipped into a few months ago was actually more complicated than I realised. I was starting to feel a bit upset that no one in the society had warned me that this was possible. Although to be honest if they had said anything I would probably have thought it was a wind up.

I still had very little clue where this was going, but I felt reassured that even if I didn't understand it that Bridget did and she would be able to handle things. I looked across at her again and smiled, she smiled back.

"Nearly there" she offered cheerfully as we crossed Lothian Road. The buzz of the traffic and the crowds of people streaming in both directions seemed reassuring. Normal. Things were still the same. I was just a bit off and it would all soon be fixed. I nodded, still not entirely sure where we were going, but happy that it wasn't too far. We soon turned off the main road and another corner over what seemed to be a bridge.

I wasn't familiar with the neighbourhood so I didn't realise until we got halfway across. I looked up to see a small huddle of cottages off to one side, I saw it and thought enclave. There was a railing marking out the edge and it seemed to immediately go from tarmac to cobbles. It was like a small section of the past had held off time from passing and was surviving by drawing a line over which change couldn't get too much of a foothold.

"My little oasis of calm" Bridget offered as we headed down between the cottages. The road took us past the colony cottages with their small gardens, some tidy, others a complete mess, but everything here, as Bridget had said, felt very calm. I could feel some of the tension leaving me as we walked further into the hidden area of peace in the city.

At the very back of the oasis there was a small single storey cottage tucked away to one side. Looking at it, I felt this was the heart of place. The reason why neither the 21st nor the 20th Century had happened yet.

The feeling of calm deepened as we passed through her garden gate. It was like the silence was so deep here you could feel it in the air.

"It's lovely" I couldn't help but say as the warm scent of roses and lilacs filled my nose as we walked down her path.

I felt like I was coming home to a strange house, but it felt wonderful. I took some deep breaths of the evening air, my pace slowing as I enjoyed the stroll between her flower beds and grass.

The door framed by a small wooden porch with a horseshoe nailed above it under layers of paint. The small grey stone cottage looked like something out of a fairytale.

"Thank you, and come on in" Bridget took the compliment with a smile, I could tell she was pleased.

We went into the dim hallway where she quickly led me into a side room which looked like a bit of a crazy space. I could just about make out a dining table at one side of the room, but it was mostly hidden under a jumble of books and bits and pieces.

I was drawn to browse the bookshelves while Bridget went and moved a few things off one of the armchairs that were set either side of a small fireplace. There wasn't any order that I could see. The books seemed to combine literature and medical texts with books on botany and herbs. I looked around the room enjoying it but feeling even more that this was becoming more like a fairy tale.

There was a dry and earthy smell in the air that was reassuring, it was coming from the herbs drying on a rack in the corner of the room. I began to wander around looking at things while Bridget continued to rearrange things by the fireplace.

Nothing seemed to match, but it was clear that everything in the room was here for a purpose. It struck me that it reflected Bridget really well, it was quirky but felt right.

"Over here, take a seat please." Bridget called me over so I stopped wandering and settled down into the seat she pointed me to. She began to light some candles and burning some incense which added to the comforting aroma in the room, but began to give it a more mystical feel. I watched her carefully, both intrigued and starting to feel a little uncomfortable. The chair was really relaxing, but gave the feeling that it was trying to swallow me whole. I struggled against it for a bit, trying to combat the feeling that I was trapped.

I glanced at the fireplace and caught myself thinking I was grateful that there wasn't a cauldron hanging over it. That might have been the final straw. I told myself I was being stupid, she wasn't the wicked witch. It was just that we had left my comfort zone behind and although candles and incense were normally fine, the mood was getting weirder again. I felt I had to try and make things more normal by chatting.

"So have you lived here long?" I tried to sound as casual as possible, and I think I managed despite my throat suddenly feeling very dry.

"Hmm?" Bridget looked up from the table obviously not quite having caught the question.

"I said, have you lived here long?" I repeated trying to rise again, but failing.

I slipped back a bit further and had to fight the odd mental image that it was like an upholstery version of a Venus Fly trap. It was going to try and dissolve me using tea and biscuits. All it wanted was for me to stop struggling.

"Oh, yeah, for a few years now. Now stop getting so restless. I need you to sit and be quiet for a bit while I get myself ready." Her tone shocked me. Having gone from such a friendly situation to being spoken to so sharply, I pushed myself back into the chair. Uncertain why things had changed so abruptly. Bridget stopped sorting things on the table and turned back around to look at me. I could see that she was regretting the tone but I wasn't sure how she would handle it.

"Okay, that was a bit like an adult addressing a problematic child, I apologise. I am just feeling distracted as I am getting together a few things that will help me. Once I've done that, what I intend to do is to take you into a very light trance and see what I can do about the 'blockage' if you are happy for me to call it that." I felt better that she had apologised, and I nodded to her that it was okay. I didn't know what to say and was a bit worried that she still had things to do and I didn't want her to mess up.

"Now sit back and relax". Bridget came over to me, put the incense burner down by the fire and began to scatter something that looked like salt and herbs around the chair.

Bridget

I got him settled in the armchair, still feeling quite pleased that he had complimented my home. It is such a special place to me that having someone feel inspired to say something nice means a lot. My nervousness however began to grow quite quickly. It was coming to the crunch time. I had decided on a plan that would allow me to learn more about him and the situation, but as ever knowing how much power he had been unconsciously throwing around, I had to take precautions and hope that it all went to plan.

I decided to focus on getting the necessary bits and pieces arranged, salt and some blessed herbs to make the circle was the simplest bit. I picked a relaxing incense as I wanted to relax myself a bit more and also create the right atmosphere. He tried speaking to me, and I did my best to focus, but ended up snapping at him as it carried on. I realised my mistake immediately and apologised to him.

I realised I was actually just delaying, the whole situation was starting to make me more concerned, but I was out of options other than giving it a go. I was sorely tempted to turn it into a more flirtatious conversation and try and distract us both, but I realised that this wasn't wise so I pushed that thought away and gathered the things that I thought would help.

I told him to "Sit back and relax" and began to prepare the space around him. The basic circle of protection that I cast around the chair helped me feel more calm.

The rituals of preparation always helped me get through moments of tension. The personal symbolism of them was where a significant part of their power lay.

I muttered to myself a little as I shaped the intention of the space, not wanting to worry him with the details of what I was doing. The twin influences of magic and psychology helped me to feel more able to handle what was coming next. The basic barrier was designed to contain the psychic energy that was going to be unleashed and also to protect against any passing external influences.

I could see that while the ritual was helping me it wasn't having the same effect on John. The practice of magic, or even basic ritual, was so alien to him it was having the opposite effect.

I decided to move up to the next level of intervention, he was going to need a bit more assistance to make him relax. I reached down and uncorked the bottle of home-brewed wine that I had collected for this purpose, and hoped would be useful. I had been careful and picked something with enough kick to loosen him up but not strong enough to get him completely drunk, my experimental home-made spirits were more along that line. I felt that the nuclear option should be avoided at this point. I handed him the glass, resisting the temptation to allow my fingers to brush his, the lure of that power was still strong. He nodded some thanks and took a cautious sip.

"Delicious." he murmured, I smiled my thanks, but kept focused on the task at hand.

I responded by beginning to talk at him in a gentle tone. Keeping it light and explaining that I needed him to relax, and that it would all be fine.

As he finished the wine, I took the glass and set it down on the floor next to the chair and began to guide him through some simple relaxation techniques. The combination of the wine and the techniques began to work and I could see the tension leaving his body. As I hoped he settled deeper down towards the trance state I was encouraging him to enter.

Once I was confident that he was ready, I began to talk him through a more formal guided meditation. I needed to create a specific mood in him for my plan to work, it was vital he be in as receptive a state as possible. I had avoided telling him I was going to use hypnosis, the preconceptions that come with that would have been difficult to counter.

I wasn't planning on making him cluck like a chicken, nor was I going to swing a pocket watch in front of his face melodramatically declaiming that he was becoming sleepy. Popular culture as ever tends to get things wrong for dramatic effect, so the best plan was just to get him to relax and do what was necessary.

I was observing him closely, initially on the physical level, but I then tuned my awareness to read his aura again. It was easier to see when he became suitably relaxed for me to move onto the next level of my plan. If he had been concerned with my other preparations, but had managed to overcome them, I was glad I hadn't explained the next bit of my plan to him either.

The majority of this first section was nothing different from what any hypnotherapist would have done, well possibly the booze excluded, but it was now going to get more mystical. I was able to get myself quickly into the correct state of mind for what I wanted to do next, which was pure witchcraft.

I asked John to visualise a room that he knew well, and where he felt comfortable and safe. As I got him to describe it to me, I used his receptive state and his own description to form a psychic connection between us. Once we connected I used my power to enhance the process so that as he described it to me it took shape. When I felt I had a clear idea of what he was describing and that he was feeling comfortable there, I went across the link I had made to join him.

Opening my eyes inside the vision I took in the details of what was there. It was obviously a bedroom that had been occupied by the same person for a long time, one who was bad at letting things go. The surfaces had clutter of different hobbies, the books on a small bookcase in the corner ranged from childhood favourites to teen fiction favourites of a couple of decades ago.

I inhaled deeply and could even pick up the slight tang of the glue from the Airfix model that was half completed on the desk, amidst other odds and sods. John was standing with his back to me looking out of the window, onto what to me looked like an idealised version of a suburban garden. The air was warm and the space felt like a safe place to just exist. I decided that while it was nice here that we didn't want to stay too long, it was just the starting point for my plan.

"Very nice!" I said letting him know I was now here. John was obviously startled, he turned around quickly and looked very confused, as if he wasn't sure who I was.

"This is a nice strong visualisation, with such a peaceful resonance. You're lucky to have this good a memory."

I moved over to join him at the window, walking slowly, allowing him to adjust again to my presence. The window had gone opaque, with now just plain warm golden light streaming through past the curtains; John was watching me closely.

I gave him a minute, and could see him recall me and accept that I was there, but I could tell he was still a bit confused.

"I'm sorry, but what is happening?" He tried shaking his head to clear it, but it didn't work. "Bridget? Why are we here? My parents moved out of this house years ago, we were just in your house. This just feels so bizarre."

The anxiety was mounting in his voice so I risked stepping closer to him, and lightly touched his arm to reassure him. Hopeful that within this construct of his memory and imagination there was less risk I would connect with the underlying power.

"It is okay. You are safe. We are here together. Everything is fine. Just take a moment and relax." I did my best to exude more calm towards him. It was vital that he didn't get agitated, as I needed to get to the root of the problem.

I believed the best plan was to get past the self-restricting habits that we place on ourselves on a daily basis. We could only do that if he stayed relaxed, and accepted that there was a level of reality to the situation that would allow it to play out naturally, rather than it being something he consciously created. It was only a little bit beyond the level of suspension of disbelief that theatre or tv shows asked of people, just enough to allow the emotions to surface and guide us through to the heart of the problem.

If he fought against me and the validity of the illusion it would be a lot harder. I made a snap decision and gave him a small nudge to reinforce the reality of the illusion that he had created for himself. I suppressed the small pang of guilt I felt, if I had been able to reason him through this I would probably have let him take more time. The intervention had the result I wanted and he appeared calmer, if a bit more distracted.

"Don't worry John, it's all fine. Everything is fine. We are just here to take a little journey. This is just the starting point." I reassured him and walked over to the door. "Come on, we need to find what I'm looking for so we can get your little problem sorted out."

I pulled open the door to reveal a simple corridor, more akin in style to a hotel than that found in a house. It stretched away into the distance, with doors appearing sporadically in the walls of different styles.

I walked with him down the corridor, looking for clues or options to see how this would unfold.

As we turned a corner I noted that on one side were four doors in the same style, very close together, coloured White, Black, Red and Blue. "Ah. You've played that game I see." I muttered, resisting the urge to peek into them. If they were relevant to the cure they would be more significant, but I knew it was just curiosity that had brought them to my attention. I had to stick more closely to my professional ethics and resolve the matter at hand.

Realising John had also stopped, he was staring at the doors and I could see he was trying to make sense of them.

I could feel his struggle against the internal logical inconsistencies of the world he was experiencing. The door we went through shouldn't have lead here, and none of what he was seeing made sense.

I felt the energy in him shift as he tried to make it make sense, and it even distorted my perception of his avatar. It rippled and fluctuated as his mind tried to work out what was actually happening. Reaching for his hand I tried to encourage him along the corridor. I could see an archway a little further along which marked the end of the corridor.

As we got closer, John mostly allowing me to guide him, I could see that there was a stone staircase ascending and descending from this point, the stone walls had a combination of electrical lights and flickering torches casting light over the scene. John stopped, and pulled his hand from my grip.

"Where are we?" his irritation and distress now apparent. He shook his head again, trying to clear it of the muddled thoughts he must be having; as he did so, the distortion spread from his body into the world surrounding us which began to lose solidity. The walls billowed briefly as if they were made of mist before re-establishing themselves as walls.

I realised that I had miscalculated and needed to reassess the situation, I realised that despite my fears and doubts about his ability to cope, there was really only one option that remained. The truth.

"We are currently inside your head, in a figurative sense." I kept my tone as level as I could.

Hoping that being matter of fact would allow him to keep himself calm and not undermine my plan. "Everything you see around us is a construct, shaped by your imagination and your subconscious. The only 'real' thing here that isn't from inside your mind is this projection of me, and I am only here at your sufferance."

I added a quick muttered "Maybe I should have explained first," more to give vent to my own frustration at my previous misplaced certainty, but it also served as a half apology to him. I searched his face looking for any reaction to what I had said. I was deeply regretting my previous assumptions that as he didn't understand magic he wouldn't be able to cope with the basic mechanics of what I was going to try and achieve with him. In a very literal sense he knew his own mind better than I did.

I gave him time to think it through and I could see in his eyes when he had pieced it all back together again. It was a combination of wonder, excitement and a bit of fear.

"So. Hang on." John began looking around us at the space. "That means..." and without him finishing the sentence the scene changed.

We were now standing in the corridor of what was obviously a school, a primary school to judge from the style and quality of the artwork that adorned the walls. Either that or it was a very avant-garde exhibition where the medium of finger painting was being taken to new levels. If the art and architecture were not enough to confirm their location, there was the smell. That distinctive school odour of the mingling of cleaning materials, PVA glue and education.

Directly in front of us sitting on the floor, hugging his knees, was a small boy. The stereotypical tousle-haired ragamuffin in physical appearance but who was observing the floor at his feet with that air of mournfulness that only small children can muster.

The unabashed display of such honest sad emotion would have only been possible in an adult under extreme circumstances, such as a bereavement. However for children, who generally feel the world more keenly, every setback in fortune, is earth shattering and doesn't need to be hidden. This perplexes adults who fail to see, or have forgotten, how the fact that there is only vanilla ice cream left rates on the same scale of trauma.

I looked over to John and guessed from his mildly deranged expression that he was having difficulty processing what he was witnessing. The similarity between his features and that of the boy made the conclusion that this was a childhood memory an easy one for me to jump to.

Before I was able to ask him anything more there was the distinctive creak of a school door and the approaching sound of sensible shoes clacking across hard linoleum. They were approaching rapidly and I looked up to see the figure turn the corner, any doubt I had previously had in my mind about the location or timing was now dispelled.

The epitome of a mid Nineteen Eighties Primary School teacher was now before us. From hairstyle, through wardrobe-that-style-has-disowned, down to the, as I suspected, very sensible court shoes.

She passed through us as if we were ghosts, without breaking her stride and came to stand before the huddled child. He had shown no signs of even hearing her approach, the misery was that all engulfing.

"Now John, I've spoken to Agnes; she told me what Ruth said, which backs up what you told me earlier." The kind tones of the teacher managed to convey compassion tinged with a hint of exasperation. I had witnessed this before in friends of mine who are currently working with small children.

I had been astounded to hear from the stories that they told me dramas which seemed to rival the plots of a grand opera. Rivalries, intrigues and passions, albeit on a smaller scale and with less sex, murder and cross-dressing, but still significant enough to make you wonder if it had been like that when I was young and I had just forgotten.

I shook my head to clear it of the musings and to focus back on the current situation. I decided I needed to talk to John again. I reached out to touch his arm.

"John. Why did you bring us here?" It was only then that I realised that he was frozen in place, his expression hadn't changed from the initial shock that he must have experienced. I began to worry that he was going to suffer some sort of breakdown. It was even more surprising when it was the child that looked up and spoke to me.

When we made eye contact the scene around us froze, the teacher now like a statue. The power of the moment was focused away from the memory and into the perpetual present.

"This was the first moment when I discovered that I could trust someone other than my family."

The boyish voice sounded odd expressing such a profound thought.

"Miss Cavendish is now going to take me back into the classroom. Ruth had been undermining me for over a year, she was a bully. I had finally snapped and pushed her; I thought I was going to be punished. Miss Cavendish gave me hope I wasn't alone."

As he finished speaking the scene around us faded into a featureless mist. I was disorientated by the sudden lack of context and was grateful that I had retained my light grip on John's arm. Even though I couldn't see anything around us, I was still able to feel him. It gave an illusion of up and down, which didn't really exist in this place, but made me feel better to retain them as reference points.

"Bridget," John said. I was reassured to hear the once again adult timbre defining the disembodied voice in the shapeless null space. "We really are in my mind, aren't we?"

"Yes. Yes we are," I confirmed for him. It was calming to be able to talk to him about it. I was getting over my initial disorientation. I felt I should try and regain an element of control over the situation.

"I need you to focus, though, I am not sure this is really helping. Can you take us back to the first corridor?"

The mist began to clear slowly, I was dismayed we were not back in the navigable corridor-construct as I had hoped, instead we were now confronted with a new scene.

This time the world gradually took shape and revealed a scene familiar to me. The suburban neighbourhood, province of the middle class and upwardly mobile.

If it had been anything like my own childhood it would be a haven of apparent family values which you learn later in life had been a cover for a lot of secret divergences.

Grey concrete slabs defined the wide pavements, and neat brick walls and trimmed hedges – the symbolic epitome of normality.

The fly in the ointment of this vision of unobjectionable mediocrity was the figure of a long-haired youth, obviously John from some point in his teenage years, lounging against said neat brick wall on a street corner.

He was dressed in that scruffy way that indicates that while the individual is rebelling, there is a respectable family somewhere behind them preventing them from going quite as far as they would otherwise. Family can sometimes provide a secure anchor against extremes of attitude or behaviour, as they know too much about how you got to where you are now. Teen-John was once again staring at his feet and was again in some obvious distress, albeit now layered with teenage concerns of not showing that fact. The gradually acquired learning of perspective and suppression of extremes of emotional reaction known as growing up was starting to take hold.

I looked around as the memory took shape and the circle of its reality widened. Figures of a more ragtag group of slightly older youths began to coalesce out of the vanishing mist a short distance away.

As they became fully real they paused and turned back towards us from what had been their obvious mob-handed departure.

Even this sudden increase in attention did nothing to remove Teen-John's focus from his deliberately scuffed, but still quite good quality trainers.

I couldn't help notice the recurring theme of self-diminution, an avoidance of engagement with the cause of discomfort. The obvious leader of the gang, as he was the scruffiest and probable winner of the 'Most likely to make parents worry if seen hanging out with their children' award, spoke.

"So, you really aren't coming then?!" The tone of challenge was clear, an ultimatum had been made and the final chance was now being offered before the door closed forever.

I couldn't help but be pulled into the moment, my concerns were shelved as I curiously watched the scene unfold. Despite my misgivings, I was enthralled at this insight into his life. I was torn between going with it and seeing if I could establish the benefit of this wander through John's memories. If I had to get us back on track I might have to take more radical action again. It was a risk but I feared it was the only way to get us closer to the answers I felt we needed.

The John I had arrived with stood passively by my side, his expression blank this time confirming that he was subsumed fully into reliving this particular memory and I was just an outside observer. The Teen-John spoke.

"Yeah. I'm not." While it was not the most coherent of rebuttals, it was accurate. I was impressed by his ability to express it with both a tone of defiance that also hinted, to a skilled observer like myself, towards the complex layers of doubt.

It was clearly a combination of uncertainty at what the actual implications were of making this decision with such a definite statement, and partly normal teenage confusion.

I turned to face the teen-aged version of John to ask my question. Having realised that within a construct you have to play by the rules even if you aren't exactly sure what they are. Thankfully I'm a quick learner.

"What did you decide not to do?" Again the scene froze, like someone had hit pause on the world for everyone except me and the version of John I had to engage with. I felt it was my only choice at this point, even though playing along with the stream of consciousness struck me as being most likely a waste of time.

I had to try, at least until I could work out how to steer it, to play along. The teenaged John looked up at me, his eyes not entirely focused, slightly red from the tears that he was about to shed and was ashamed to acknowledge.

"This was when I decided not to run away with my friends to an eco-camp in Wales. We had all sworn to try and fix all of the world's problems by dropping out of the system. Donny, the loud one, had this uncle out there who would help us get started, and train us as true eco-warriors.

Instead, I spent the summer working as a temp in my Dad's office. Went on and got my 'A' levels, and then went to Uni. I never saw any of that crowd again.

We had tried so hard to prove that the world was being ruined, and all I could see was the fear in my parents' eyes that I would end up a homeless drifter.

I couldn't match the passion that the other guys had for it, so I stopped. Stopped worrying about things I couldn't fix and stuck to what was in front of me. It was easier to stop caring totally than to try and balance out the mainstream and extreme."

It confirmed to me that I suspected his subconscious was trying to play out for me the entire sequence of life events that had led us to this point. He was trying to set out the context for the current problem, while I could see this had some benefit, I was painfully aware that I was not a psychologist, and this rehearsal of contributory factors could take a very long time.

My skills in this area were more geared towards the magical, rather than the medical. I could try and develop my understanding but it felt much more intrusive than I was hoping for, having John's entire subconscious laid bare to me like this was not the solution I felt was best. I decided to see if I could help him find a shortcut.

The scene began to fade back to the gray mist again, this was my opportunity. I stepped back to grab the arm of the 'current' John and held tight. Trying to not let the concern that I was feeling that we would be stuck in this process for a long time manifest in my voice, other than to give strength to the tone of command that I used.

"Listen to me, this is important. I understand what you are showing me, I get the importance of this, but I don't think we have time for this right now." I paused, hoping that I had broken through into his awareness. The recollection process was too immersive in any of the relived memories. I was very relieved when I heard his voice come back to me,

"What do you need me to do then?" he sounded like it was a struggle to talk, but it was clear he was once again in control of the process. The grey nothingness that surrounded us made it hard for me to remain calm.

A complete absence of reference points is disorientating, including the absence of a heart beat to even give a pretence of the passing of actual time. I was terrified that if I didn't keep him focused we could end up lost in his subconscious. I prayed to whatever deities or forces could hear me in this unusual place and did my best to phrase the request as precisely as I could.

"What I need you to do is take me to where you feel the pressure is growing. That will be the power that flowed through you when the other incidents happened." I held the illusion of my breath as it made me feel better to continue to act as if I was still operating in a real body.

The mist began to swirl around us. I let myself breathe again. It was still amorphous but there was a distinct impression of movement that reassured me. I began to feel more pressure under my fingers, as if his arm was taking on more substance. I squeezed it gently in the hope that he could feel it too and I was positively reinforcing what was happening.

The mist began to take on form, the corridor in which we had begun our journey was taking shape. It didn't return to the full colour and quality it had before, it stayed indistinct but was a welcome point of reference. I tried to take a step and realised I couldn't, we were actually floating a few inches above the 'ground'. And while I felt supported and safe I couldn't get myself to move.

It made me feel a little like a ghost.

This immobility didn't last long, but it was driven by John's mind. We began to float down the corridor towards the archway that contained the stairway that lead downwards. Our speed began to increase but was not combined with any sense of motion which started to induce an inverted form of travel sickness. The details of the walls became harder to pay attention to, so I shifted my focus to John, he looked calm but determined, but was again seemingly unresponsive to my presence.

The optical effect of moving stopped abruptly and I was again aware that we had a firm floor beneath our feet. Colour quickly returned to the world around us, spreading out in a wave as the area gained substance from our presence. I glanced back and saw that we were at the foot of the stairs, ahead of us a roughly hewn corridor led a short distance to another archway.

The bright light from 'outside' was dazzling so I couldn't make out what lay ahead of us. John paused just ahead of me, silhouetted against the light. I couldn't tell if he needed more prompting or not, I decided to try.

"On we go then." I felt was appropriate encouragement. I stepped closer, relieved to find that I could move again, but aware that I didn't want to crowd him.

I was torn between curiosity to see what shape the solution would take. Anxious that it was going to be beyond my ability to interact with this situation properly. He started walking forward and I followed close behind.

During the trip down memory lane, even with the bizarre qualities of how we got there, everything about the scenes had felt 'real' and 'normal' so I wasn't quite prepared for what now appeared before me.

The space we had come out into was at first impression a huge garden, but I then realised it was actually a giant greenhouse, beyond the scale even of the ones at the Royal Botanic Gardens. That was not the oddest thing, that award went to the quality of the environment.

Everything here felt it was trying too hard. All the colours were too bright, the edges too sharp, the shadows too deep. As I stepped further out from the stairwell, I was hit by the heat. It was oppressive. I mopped my brow half expecting to be sweating but I was still dry.

Once I got over the original shock, the space was not that impressive, despite its size. It was quite banal. There was a gently undulating lawn of grass, it reminded me of an extensive, but not particularly well cared-for suburban garden. All that was missing to complete that impression was a section of patio or decking.

The only feature which provided any relief was a small section of slightly wonky trellis that had some vines growing over it. As I looked around, possibly coming into being as I observed them, I started noticing small flowerbeds and shrubs in the distance. Most of them looked particularly unhealthy and the intensity of the colours and contrast only served to make this more obvious.

It felt like the type of space that a garden makeover programme would regard as a good project and would want to add some 'pizazz' or something equally irritating. What it needed was proper care, as a keen gardener I knew what it was lacking. Some care and attention.

I pushed these thoughts away. Despite not sweating the oppressive heat was getting to me and I was allowing my mind to focus on irrelevancies, rather than the challenge at hand. I began to start looking at all of these things as clues. The state of care was probably just a symptom of the wider situation and less likely to be the cause.

I wandered further into the space, the glass roof overhead was dirty. Probably just another sign of neglect and not feeling like the key to the problem. As I walked further away from the archway that stood incongruously in the middle of the garden, showing no sign of the stairwell above it, I nearly tripped into a small stream. It had been so small I didn't see it until I was right on top of it. I should have realised that there would be a water feature.

I followed it and found quickly that it ended in a large muddy puddle right at the small wall that marked the edge of the greenhouse. It was as large as the pond we had in my garden as a child, I guessed it would only come up to my waist if I were to get into it.

The water was murky and uninviting so I wasn't thinking that was likely. I looked around and realised that the stream I followed was not the only one. There was actually a network of tiny streams all flowing through the garden and terminating at this point, they were well hidden by the undulating quality of the ground. Ubiquitous but mostly unnoticed.

This was starting to feel more like the type of thing that could be fixed, and obvious problem to which we might be able to make a solution. There were no other puddles or ponds, so I guessed that the streams must all meet here and there was something making the water backup and create the puddle. It was obvious from the uneven shape and the damaged state of the plants and grass around the edge that despite my original thought about water features this was not a design feature of the space.

I looked around and John was ambling slowly towards me, stepping over the streams and only occasionally seeming to notice any of the flowers or plants that grew around. I was trying to not jump to the obvious conclusion but it felt right, I decided to wait until John joined me.

"Now this is a fine mess, you've gotten me into." I couldn't help but mutter to myself. The blockage was obviously somewhere under the water, and I suspected I was going to have to get more hands-on than I wanted.

I didn't know the rules of the construct yet, but if that water was a symbol of the problem I was not looking forward to getting into it myself. There were always going to be twists and turns when dealing with a world created from a combination of psychology and magic - neither was particularly good at only ever being what it appeared on the surface.

I stepped back and tried to be rational about it all.

The heat was oppressive, possibly because I wasn't feeling the relief that would have come if I had been able to have the illusion of sweat. I tried to will myself cooler, but as we were in John's mind I was effectively powerless unless I wanted to try something dramatic, and that would have been dangerous so just had to tolerate the discomfort.

I squinted up towards the glass roof, that might be part of the problem, was this magical 'hot-housing'? I looked around and there didn't seem to be any solution on that level. Breaking the glass would not be wise, again it could cause dangerous trauma to John, as I wasn't clear on what it represented and it would need to be his actions and choices that made any changes down here.

Having put that from my mind, I was drawn again to the obvious answer - it was to do with the water and the puddle. I felt doubtful, it couldn't really be that simple? I was getting pulled into a cycle of suspicion and doubt and the heat was making it harder and harder for me to think. John had now joined me and was staring fascinated at the murky waters of the pond.

"So have you noticed anything?" I asked hoping that this would get the process started again. He looked briefly confused, his mind ironically was elsewhere. After a moment he pulled his focus from the water and made eye contact with me.

"Huh? Oh yeah, this pond looks wrong, but the vine on the trellis is doing really well." He nodded his head back towards the trellis, which had been on the other side of the archway to the pond.

"Okay, tell me what you noticed." I asked and began to wander back towards the archway, feeling more lethargic as we went. He was right, of all the plants in the garden the vine was definitely doing the best. As we got closer I saw that some of the tendrils were working along the ground towards the archway, but hadn't quite reached it.

"There seems to be grapes." John added, coming close behind me. He was also seeming to show signs of the heat getting to him, but he was actually sweating. I had never envied anyone that before, but that was the difficulty of being in a magical construct that was part of someone else's mind, the rules were not consistent.

I took a closer look and indeed hidden under the large leaves on certain areas there were large purple grapes hanging in clusters. I looked at them and tried to establish their connection to all of this, I was feeling more tired and the trellis wasn't giving me anything. It felt like this was again a symptom and not a cause.

"What do you think?" I asked pointlessly wiping my dry forehead and focusing on trying to understand the situation.

"I think the pond is wrong." John said and turned and began to walk back towards it. I followed behind, uncertain of what else I could do. His instincts and mine agreed that the water was the obvious problem. I still didn't trust it, but I was running out of options.

"Okay then. The pond it is."

I joined him at the edge of the water again. It was both wonderful in its simplicity but had such potential for complexity.

The adage about still waters came to mind and were never deemed to always be safe.

I decided to try one last thing before moving forward.

I adjusted my perceptions to sustain my connection with the world he had created but to try and make sense of it on the level where I could perceive the natural flows of energy as colour and shapes.

I normally much preferred that as it was down to my ability to interpret what I saw and didn't have this extra layer of another person's psychology colouring it. I was briefly staggered and nearly blinded by what I saw. The conflicting chaos of colour and movement with the intensity were more than I could handle. I quickly shifted back and hoped that I wasn't going to get a migraine from even the brief exposure. It had been nearly overwhelming.

My options were limited. We would have to work within the constraints of the narrative version that his mind had created. It seemed that we would have to manually unblock the stream, which I hoped in turn would resolve the problem as it was manifesting in the real world.

"So. We agree the pond is wrong. What needs to be done? Can you tell me anything more?" I was determined to now try and lead him towards fixing things. My normal instinct to just fix things was not going to work here. I was acting blind to the underlying forces that were at work so I had to operate on the visible level.

It was sometimes the case that if you pushed hard at one spot you could end up having something apparently unconnected push back harder. The normal rules of cause and effect tended not to follow when dealing with the magical and psychic realms. It was like using a see-saw that had been designed by Escher.

"I think so," the effort of speaking was apparently now quite great. The sweat was dripping from his face and the heat seemed to be slowing his thoughts down. We had made it back to the pond and it was drawing all of his attention so my question was pulling him away from something a lot stronger. I gave him space to continue.

"There's a blockage over there by the wall where the water heads out. I think I need to go and see what's causing the problem." He continued looking but managed to vaguely point into the dark water ahead of us. I let him carry on, it seemed the best option.

As he entered the water I heard him gasp from what I presumed was the cold but that sound was quickly drowned out by the sudden roaring of water that now filled the air. My perception of the situation suddenly changed. The small stream was now transformed into a raging torrent and the gentle grassy lawn was now a landscape of rocky crags and ancient wild forests. From my vantage point on the high bank I could just see John being pulled down into the water, white spray filling the air as he quickly disappeared into the torrent.

Overcoming my initial shock at the change I began shouting his name and started to work my way towards the edge. I thought I could climb down the cliff that now separated me from where I had seen him pulled under the water. My movements became sluggish, it was taking more and more effort for me to make any progress. The pressure increased around him and my sight began to dim. I cried out his name one more time and then with the sudden sensation of rapid acceleration I felt myself being thrown upwards and everything went black.

John

It was odd how easy I had found it to accept that we were in my mind. After the initial confusion I was able to mentally go 'oh okay'. Once I had Bridget's presence and the way things felt it just made sense. Popping back into those specific memories had been very uncomfortable. I was actually relieved when Bridget told me to move away from them. I could tell there was more that was going to follow, but with a bit of effort I had been able to pull us out. The request to find the pressure made sense. It was like an aching muscle that was outside of my body, but I could still feel it. It was really odd.

As we reached the garden, which I'd never seen before but was familiar, the sensation grew stronger. I was still trying to work it out when Bridget called me over. The heat was making it even harder for me to focus. So I just let myself wander around, feeling a bit like I was playing blind man's buff, although the silent signals weren't 'hotter' and 'colder' just 'wrong' and 'less wrong'.

The pond was definitely the centre of the 'wrong' feeling. It was like looking at your face and seeing something was wrong and only slowly working out that you had someone else's nose. The odd thing was I knew I had never seen it before, so I couldn't work out how I knew it was wrong.

What I also couldn't work out is how it was possible that Bridget wasn't sweating like I was, it was obviously hot but she looked dry where I was dripping.

She kept on asking me questions but I couldn't really focus on her. The wrongness of the pond was getting stronger and was filling my mind.

She asked me what needed to be done, and I could see the solution as she asked me, although I still had no idea why. It just sort of made sense.

She told me to go and sort it out so I waded into the water. It was so cold I gasped. My head cleared instantly, I felt able to think again. I had either adapted really quickly or the water had changed temperature with me. It now felt great and I didn't mind the fact I was fully clothed. I looked around, seeing if Bridget was going to join me or tell me what to do next. She wasn't there.

"Bridget?" I called out. Although there was nowhere she could have gone that was out of sight in the short time I had turned my back. None of the plants were big enough to hide her and the door was too far away. The fact that she had disappeared worried me a little bit, but I was starting to feel much better in general. I also reckoned that of the two of us, she was more able to look after herself in weird situations. I shrugged and decided to carry on with the last plan.

Maybe she thought she was done and it was now up to me to sort this out, now that she had brought me here.

There was a stillness to this greenhouse garden thing that despite the oddness I found reassuring. I realised in a very literal sense I was alone with my thoughts. I chuckled to myself and turned to start wading further into the pond.

Losing my footing I panicked for a second, all my flailing did was make the splash that little bit bigger. Thankfully it wasn't a deep pond and I was able to struggle back onto my feet. Dripping wet but in no apparent danger of drowning. The ducking actually made me feel happier. I laughed at myself. It was ridiculous but fun.

I shook my head to get the water out of my ears and hair and began to more cautiously wade towards the wall. As I got to the wall the depth was still only just above waist deep so I wasn't feeling it was too dangerous. I reached down to feel under the surface to work out what was blocking the way. There was mud. I pulled a handful out and brought it to the surface, it was smooth and felt really nice to touch.

As I rubbed it between my fingers a slight whiff of decay came from it, but not an unpleasant one. It was just a reminder that things die to feed new life. Not knowing what else to do I began to reach more deeply into the mud, trying to find what was holding it all together. Something more substantial had to be in there causing the blockage.

Bridget

The first thing I became aware of was the foul taste in my mouth. The return to consciousness was slow and very painful. The internal cataloguing of discomforts continued and was rapidly crowned by the awareness that I had a pounding headache. I turned my head slowly and opened one eye, the light coming in through the gap in the curtains was like a lance stabbing deep into my skull. I muttered a few choice curses and closed my eye to allow that particular pain to subside.

After a minute or so of slow breathing and mustering my self discipline I had gotten myself under better control. It was progress but I was still feeling like something dead that had been bullied back into a semblance of life. I hadn't felt this bad for a long time, it wasn't common but any magic that went wrong could easily leave you with a hangover that made those caused by even the roughest alcohol feel like a slight tickle behind the eyes in comparison. I hoped that John was in better shape. I still didn't know exactly what had caused that change but it might have affected him worse.

I squinted up at where I had left him. The seat was empty. In surprise I opened both eyes, and the increase in light made the pain increase again. Gritting my teeth I began to look around. There was no sign of him in the room. I listened carefully, but there were no telltale sounds of anyone else in the cottage. Forcing myself to swallow a few times to get my throat working I just managed to croak out his name. I waited a few moment but there was no response.

"Oh crap". I moaned. Lowering myself back down on to the carpet I rested my head in my hands and steeled myself for whatever was going to happen next.

After I had searched the cottage and found no sign of him, I retreated to the kitchen and treated my own trauma the best I could. It wasn't until I was ladling sugar into my second mug of coffee, and eating the last biscuits that I felt able to even start working out what might have happened. I had already, quite shamefully, checked to ensure that there wasn't a small pile of ash or a charred outline on the armchair. Things hadn't gone that badly wrong.

I knew what I had seen, what I had felt, but I still hadn't quite made sense of it all. I realised that I needed backup. I needed a friend. I knew exactly which one. I needed the particular friend who had gotten me into this. I reached for the phone and stifled the groan that this apparently entirely unreasonable request that I made of my body elicited. I would have to ask the friend to bring painkillers.

Maebh

The noise kept on. I had to do something. It took me three goes to get my phone both the right way up and near my ear. It was definitely one of those mornings. No one sane would be calling me this early on a Saturday morning. I grunted into the phone and listened to the voice on the other end. It took me a little bit to realise it was Bridget on the other end. I started bullying my grey matter into paying attention. Something wasn't right.

"Bridget? Is that really you? You sound truly awful." I struggled into the best version of awake I could manage.

"Get over here, and pick up some aspirin on your way. And don't you dare get caught up by any random projects between here and there! You're needed and it's urgent." Bridget's had a talent for pitching her voice to exactly communicate her mood. I had never heard this combination of tiredness and pissed-offness before. She was a class act. I found myself already swinging my feet out of bed even before I had fully decided to go.

"See you soon." I told her sighing as I hung up the phone. This was not the plan. It was most definitely not the plan. I looked over and was grateful that the call and conversation hadn't woken Jo, so I did my best to slip out of bed without causing too much more disruption. The best laid plans and all that meant that I ended up stubbing my toe on the bedroom door after I got dressed. The initial yelp made them stir and they were then treated to a stream of muttered, but very expressive, words. I hobbled out of the flat and down the stairs of the tenement.

Getting outside I was pleasantly surprised at how gorgeous the morning was. The summer so far had been on the poor side of 'Scottish' for a few weeks and all reports had indicated that was set to continue. Looking up, the sky was a beautiful blue, it was an unusual shade. Something about it kept pulling my eyes. Popping into the corner shop for the aspirin and few other bits and pieces I decided to do a quick poll.

"Do you think the sky is more cyan or azure today?" The look of confusion from the young laddie behind the counter made me realise that it was still too early for such questions.

"It's blue. Is there anything else?" The polite formality of the second request made it clear I was not going to get a debate on the application of two of my favourite and underused words.

"Nope, that's all. Cheerie bye." I quickly stepped out again wanting to get back to enjoying the beauty of the sky. The more I looked at it, the more it made me feel that it wasn't normal for Scotland. I was getting thoughts of sandy deserts baked under hundred of years of heat. Which isn't part of the normal soft warmth, gentle light and midges. The temperature was starting to rise. I was grateful I had dressed in a rush as I was in my comfortable floaty stuff. It is what I wore around the house and was well suited to higher temperatures.

It was starting to feel like Scotland had been shipped down to the Mediterranean overnight. As much as we joked about it, it wasn't that likely.

A gentle breeze stirred the trees as I crossed Melville Drive and stepped out onto the green expanse of the Meadows. I love living so close to them. This and the other parks dotted around the city make Edinburgh such a fabulous place to live. It brings nature into the city, reminds us of our roots. As I stepped off the tarmac and onto the grass I could feel the energy surging in the ground. Things felt more alive today than they had been yesterday.

My heart began to beat faster in response to the energy below my feet. My whole body began to resonate. It felt fantastic. I opened up my awareness to appreciate the feeling. It served to enhance the connection, one of the perks of being a Witch is being able to feel the natural world more keenly. Pausing for a second I slipped off my sandals so I could walk barefoot on the grass and really enjoy this unexpected surge of power.

Walking further across the meadows directly across the grass was the best path for time and for pleasure, the grass gently caressing my feet and ankles. The velvety coolness of the dewy stalks on my skin was almost erotic, particularly when layered against the surging power I could feel from the earth. The pain from my stubbed toe quickly faded, replaced by pleasurable tingling that spread up from the ground, echoing with every step.

It wasn't normal, this much energy.

Even for summer it was unusually active. I started paying attention to it, reaching out my awareness to see if there were any clues. It was wrong. It was far too strong.

Looking down as I walked I thought it was an optical illusion, just caused by the angle of my head and the summer sun, it wasn't. The grass was growing. Quickly. I looked back along my path and the route I had followed was marked by a visibly higher strip of grass. The joy that I had felt disappeared. I kept walking. Not wanting to stop. Not daring to. I had to get off the grass. I quickened my pace. I don't know whether it read my mind or just responded to my faster walking but the grass sped up as well.

It began to twine and twist around my ankles.

Pulling at me.

I ran.

Panic driving me forward.

Nearing the path one of the trees closest to me began to sway. Its lower branches were moving against the wind. It was reaching for me, offering a twiggy embrace.

Hippy I may be but literal tree hugging was not on my plan. Particularly when I didn't consent. Judging the movement of the branches, I spotted a shrinking gap.

I sped up, and threw myself forward. Not having done much acrobatics, my hope that I was as graceful as a ninja was probably not the case. I however impressed myself by actually making the gap and not falling flat on my face.

It might not have been the most graceful move, but I had made it. Elegant as a swan, my arse. I lay on the tarmac for a couple of seconds catching my breath and clutching my sandals and shopping bag to my chest.

Willing my heart to slow down, I decided I had to keep moving. I might not actually be safe.

Standing carefully keeping an eye on the tree it seemed it was now dormant. The rising crest of grass stood like a frozen green tsunami outlining my escape trajectory. I nodded to myself; if my old P.E. teacher could have seen me now, I would still have resented them, but I could show that I wasn't the useless numpty I had been at school. I peered at the trees nearby, even though they weren't moving I was convinced that they were watching me. It was creepy.

Any earlier pleasure in the surge of power that I had connected to was gone. I was reminded that while I enjoyed the power, it was also dangerous. More dangerous when it was someone else's and it was on the attack. The first tickle of fear made me shiver. Scanning the Meadows I couldn't see anyone else around, and more positively nor any sign of additional grass growth that would show anyone else being attacked. I had to get to Bridget. If this was the reason she needed me that was good enough, and if she didn't know about this we had more problems to handle!

Slipping my sandals back on, I kept a weather eye on the grass and the trees. They stayed still but I no longer trusted them. Riding the adrenaline still running around my system I set off at a brisk pace. Keeping my eyes open for anything else waiting to creep up on me.

Making it safely to Bridget's I had worked myself up a bit on the way. I'd been running it over in my mind how I was going to tell her. I didn't open with the best possible line.

"It looked expectant. Trees shouldn't look expectant. What expectations could a tree have for goodness sake?"

Bridget however seemed to take this statement at face value and didn't challenge me for an explanation. With a wee nod, she signalled me to follow her indoors. She was looking quite worn for the start of a weekend. I had a good head of steam going and had to let it out so continued with my comments about how unreasonable it was for plants to be causing problems for people. It was only when she had taken the shopping bag from me and I had settled at the kitchen table that she spoke.

"Something happened on the way here then?" Having calmed myself down a bit, I picked up on the slightly pained sarcasm in her voice. I realised I hadn't actually explained anything to her. I took a deep breath and ran my hands over her 'distressed' kitchen table. Feeling the texture soothing my nerves by bringing me into the here and now.

I thought it was actually closer to tortured than distressed, but that is what happens when generations of witches have used the same table. It was definitely robust, and had stayed in exactly the same spot for a long time. As someone who had helped Bridget move it once, it was also possible to describe it as 'bloody heavy'.

"Hah!" Bridget's small sound of triumph brought me back from my little diversion. She was apparently very happy to find the aspirin. Which was odd as she normally didn't bother with artificial painkillers.

"So. Right. Yes." I had gotten my train of thought back on track and felt able to now tell her what had happened. Leaving the commentary side of it to later. Now I was calmer, my brush with over enthusiastic grass and trees felt a bit silly.

The manifestation wasn't innately dangerous but it definitely pointed towards some serious power and a potentially bad intent. I watched Bridget closely and could tell that she definitely needed those painkillers. Despite her rocky condition, I could tell she was absorbing what I was telling her and that she really didn't like it.

"Already...? Oh great." Bridget interjected before taking a sip of her coffee and pulling a disappointed face before downing the contents of her cup. She then stood and began to get the bits out to make a fresh pot. Her expression showed me that she was processing what she had heard. The comment however made it very clear I didn't have all of the information.

"Already?" I had to ask. When she wasn't forthcoming with more details, I expressed my disbelief that there was more to this situation that she wasn't telling me. I made it very clear that I expected a better level of disclosure from my friend.

She picked up on my interrogative tone and paused in the middle of spooning coffee into the cafetiere. I had pushed too hard. Her metaphorical hackles were up. Time to calm it down a bit more.

Realising that as I didn't know what had happened, I wasn't best placed to judge how it was best for her to tell me. I took a different tack. Bridget could be a bit prickly at times and this situation had obviously unnerved her. She wasn't going to be at her best.

"So, I am guessing you know something more about this than I do. Would you please enlighten me?" I tried to keep the sarcasm out of my tone, but only partially managed. Thankfully the rest of it was enough to soothe Bridget's ruffled feathers. I took a biscuit from the packet and used it to stop me from saying anything else.

After a moment's pause, Bridget began telling me about how she had been contacted by John, and how that had unfolded. I could tell from some of her pauses that she was editing it as we went and hadn't decided to tell me everything. The way in which she touched her hair when she mentioned John made me wonder if there was something more personal that had happened.

Little tells are always fun to watch. It had been a crammed few hours. But as it had been so busy I thought it was unlikely. Bridget wasn't the sort to let herself get foolish over a pretty face. I ruefully added to myself that this was much more my own style.

The internal monologue stopped me from interrupting Bridget, but I was still listening. Given her frosty reaction to my earlier comment, it was best to keep my mouth shut.

As she spoke I could see that some of the tension was leaving her. Sadly that didn't necessarily mean that it was all sorted, in fact the more I heard the more I realised that things were getting dangerously out of hand.

I was a bit surprised. During my meetings with John I hadn't picked up on the power being that out of control. And Beltane hadn't been any more mystical this year than before. Something had been going on there, but not this! Bridget's story was definitely worrying, as any magical working that ended with a mysterious disappearance generally wasn't going to end with rainbows and puppies.

What I didn't let on to her was how impressed I was with her skill. The visualisation trick was one that I filed away in my mind for future use.

We all had our own strengths, and my intuition had told me to pass this particular case onto Bridget rather than to try and handle it myself.

Bridget lapsed into silence following the bit where she had called me. Giving her a moment I schooled my thoughts and worked out what I felt were the most important questions to ask. The situation felt urgent, but it also felt important for us to work out what had actually happened.

John

After a while of blindly sweeping my arms through the mud, I stuck my hands deeper into the mud again; this time I felt something. The mud had been letting me move my arms through it but any attempts to just pull the wall to pieces hadn't worked, it seemed to ooze back into place immediately. It was odd: the brick wall marking the edges of the green house was only a few inches away but I was able to get my arm into the mud up to my elbow and not feel anything stopping me. I hadn't tried going any deeper.

This time on another sweep I brushed the edge of something with my fingertips. I stopped moving. I focused all my attention on the faint hints that I was getting, slowly working out the edges. Inching my hands to be able to get a good grip, having gotten both hands on it. It felt hard. Maybe a stone? I braced my legs ready to use all my strength to get it out of the mud. I heaved. It came out smoothly and so quickly I stumbled backwards. Narrowly avoiding another ducking. It was not a stone.

It was a shallow rectangle, about a foot across and a couple of inches deep.

As I moved my hands over it and removed the thin coating of mud I could feel that it was plastic. I recognised it even before I had gotten it completely clean. It was a laptop. Not just any laptop. It was my old work laptop, from my last job down south. I rinsed my hands in the water and waded back to the edge.

Climbing out of the water, I felt the temperature go up a bit again, and decided to take my shirt off so it could dry when it wasn't clinging to my body. The water quickly evaporated from my skin and it felt great to have the sun gently warming me.

Looking at the laptop. I couldn't help by wonder out loud. "What's this doing here?" I didn't feel self conscious at all about talking to myself until a faintly patronising voice came from behind me.

"That's what you need to work out."

Green-John

PAIN.

The world became nothing but pain.

BROKEN.

Torn free I floated in this constant shifting tide of overwhelming sensation.

PANIC.
FLEE.

I found the shortest route back to safety.

HOME.
SAFE.

The pain followed but was less.

HEAL.
SLEEP.

I let the safe darkness surround me and waited for the morning.

LIGHT.
SEE.

Opening my eyes felt odd.
It was so quiet.
Not just outside, but inside.
Inside my head.
The nagging had stopped.

Now what?

FOOD.

and then?

RESTLESS.
CHANGE.

Bridget

"So, when you touched John you saw something. Something that looked like Cernunnos?" Maebh asked me putting down her coffee mug and reaching for a biscuit, a new packet had been extricated from her shopping bag soon after the aspirin. I sat and rubbed my temple, relieved that the painkillers were taking effect; the aspirin and the comfort food were numbing my suffering down to a manageable level.

"Yes. That's what I saw." I was uncertain where she was going to take this, but was only echoing back what I had told her so far.

"Interesting. I really didn't get that strong a vibe from him." Maebh said, shaking her head. "I mean there was definitely some weird energy thing going on, and he was definitely freaking out when he fled Calton Hill."

I watched Maebh closely as she idly straightened the bits and pieces on the kitchen table in front of her. I could tell that she was avoiding approaching this head on. I was starting to feel well enough to notice the classic displacement activity. She generally wasn't that interested in the geometry of mugs and plates on tables. So something else had to be going on in the background.

"You only saw him when he was leaving, having missed the main show – by your own admission." I responded, not wishing to get into a comparison of our psychic capabilities, it seemed best to just contextualise it.

"Each of these events, or manifestations, would have reduced the backlog of energy so you would have met him in a more dormant phase."

I watched Maebh to see how she handled this counter position; she obviously wasn't entirely happy with my theory about a partial possession. She seemed to take this on board, but was still poking around at it. I could tell. You could almost hear the cogs whirring away.

"But still," Maebh countered, "What you are describing sounds like some sort of possession. You know how I feel about that. The early Christian church did so much to paint the older gods as demons that just throwing words like that around feels like we are supporting them. The priest of the church that I grew up in was all over that hellfire and brimstone and witchy temptresses rubbish."

I watched her closely; the aspirin had kicked in and I was feeling much better. I realised that this was hitting lots of buttons for her, she had previously described herself as "Not so much a lapsed Catholic as a levelled one."

I hadn't pointed out to her that this meant the foundations were still down there. The distaste that was clear in her voice made me wary to push her further, although I was sorely tempted. She wasn't taking my experiences seriously and that made me quite angry. I decided to let her know when she carried on quite quickly with a question.

"I am not doubting that you saw what you saw, but does it have to mean what you think it means?" That made me stop. Had I jumped to a hasty conclusion?

What if what I had seen wasn't the whole story. Being both a Witch and a Doctor for years, I had seen enough things to realise that what you see sometimes isn't what it would appear to be at first glance. I let myself wander off down this new train of thought. It was intriguing.

Where could I see that I had allowed myself to judge before fully knowing? Where could I have misinterpreted things? I had seen other people tie themselves in knots with self-doubt, but I found it quite refreshing to be able to critique my own thought processes.

"Bridget?" Maebh was trying to get my attention, but I needed to get my thoughts in order again. It was so much easier when not fighting the triple threat of headache, dehydration and a blood sugar level that had been wiped out by the exertions of quite deep magic. However I still needed a little time to think.

I looked over to her and smiled. "Hang on. Just need to get a few things straight in my head and then we can get into this in more depth." I started pacing up and down the kitchen, allowing my mind to work things over. Maebh sat and watched me, sipping her coffee and seemingly willing to wait for me to get my thoughts sorted out.

John

I froze, trying to workout if this was a likely threat. We were inside my head. It wasn't Bridget's voice. So who could it be? I hadn't heard anyone approaching, but I had been so involved in getting things out of the mud that I might have missed something. I cautiously looked back over my right shoulder.

"Hello?"

There was no one there. There was however while I was looking, a small puff of smoke, some twinkly music, and a figure appeared floating by my shoulder.

An angel.

Wings, Halo, Harp, flowing white robe. Very pale skin. Admittedly only about nine inches tall but an honest-to-goodness angel.

"You are here to work this out. The rules are being broken. You aren't supposed to be here like this. Get on with it!" The tone continued to be one of condescension although the last sentence had a hint of irritation. It seems that angels are not always sweet.

I had just pulled my old work laptop out of the mud in a greenhouse that didn't exist after walking through my childhood memories with a GP who had told me that not only was magic real but she was also a witch before she disappeared. A nine inch high angel with an attitude problem was not up there with the weirdest things of the day. I might as well go with it.

"Okay, so what do I do with this?"

A small thunderclap came from my other side. I turned to see what had caused it. I was not at all surprised when I saw a nine inch high devil floating by my left shoulder. Horns, pitchfork, goat-legs, goatee beard and deep crimson skin colour on his bare chest and other exposed skin. Yep. All normal. He was the one who decided to answer my question.

"Nothing, you don't need to do anything. Oh, maybe see if it has Solitaire on there and go and play with yourself for a bit and we'll see you later." The words were friendly but the tone was not a nice one. There was a grating quality to it that put my teeth on edge.

I looked backwards and forwards between them and then leant back so I wasn't having to turn my back to either of them. They floated forwards as well so they were both in front of me, but still at a safe distance from each other. I ran my hands over the laptop.

"Do you know I hated this thing. So many nights spent working to deadlines, weekends destroyed by not being able to feel that I could safely switch it off for more than a short while. I came so close to chucking it out of the window, so very many times. The temptation to 'accidentally' drop the blasted thing never really left me.

The day I left and handed it back was one of the best of my life. I never thought I would see it again."

It felt natural sharing the context with my new companions. It made more sense than talking to myself.

A deep repressed sequence of muscle memory kicked in and without really thinking about it I had flipped the lid open and pressed the power button.

Nothing happened.

The mixture of relief that I wasn't going to have to log in again and fear that I wasn't making progress was tough to swallow. The words to express it going the same way.

I looked up at my guests, they were just idly floating there. They were a bit ridiculous, but made sense in some way. I've never been a very religious man, we went to church a bit when I was a kid, but not for long. Still, I didn't believe that this angel would give me good moral guidance, and my doubts about how far I should trust the devil in front of me came more from common sense than any belief that this was an actually embodiment of evil. I didn't have many choices, but I felt it might be interesting to see what they said to me. The laptop lay inert in my hands, still not giving up its secrets.

Bridget

"You'll agree that there is definitely a magical energy disturbance. One that is almost conclusively linked to the Green Man energy?" I asked Maebh "Furthermore this energy disturbance is clearly centred on John." She nodded to each of these points. I found her agreement encouraging. So far so good.

Having heard her side of things as well, it made my belief that this was the underlying cause even more certain. The way that the grass and trees had responded to her opening herself up to the energy seemed to reinforce this.

"And will you agree that I perceived the energy disturbance as a manifested avatar of Cernunnos, as the Green Man? In my vision that saw it overlayed on the body of John?" I waited to see if she would object, this time the nod that came was more reluctant. Something was building in her mind, she was not often quiet for as long as she had been today.

"So having established that, what is your objection to my 'possession' theory?" I decided to open it up to her side of things, to see what she would bring to the discussion. I generally enjoyed things of this nature, and Maebh was good at debate. She paused to gather her thoughts for a moment.

"Well, my 'objection' is the implied ill intent of the possessing 'spirit'. Possession is a violent act. This pattern doesn't fit with my experience of the Green Man nor does it fit with his history. Avatars have existed, but they are normally only there if invited, or coaxed."

I nodded to show that I was open to her going into a bit more detail with her counter theory.

"It doesn't sound to me like the actual consciousness of the god is in him. He is not being controlled in that way from what you said about your interactions. Also the mood-linked stuff seems to be very human and very much John-centric; isn't it possible that he is just a very powerful, newly awakened, warlock?" Maebh finished with a hand gesture to show that she had concluded her statement and was ready to hear my thoughts.

"Okay. Apart from that dreadful word, you know I hate the term 'warlock', you really should look at the history of a word before you choose to use it so freely, it is a bit more complicated. A lot of things would fit the view that he was a Witch, but only if he were more aware of what he was doing. Even people who are very newly awakened to their powers have a little niggle of awareness, it comes with the territory.

I'll concede that it does take a little while to separate impulse from will, but it happens more quickly in the more powerful ones, that is basic survival. The level of power he is exhibiting would make him one of the most magically powerful people I've ever met, or even heard about. He is not even comparable to a force ten gale, he is basically a magical super storm.

So if it was genuinely coming from within his own mind, the control should have come quickly too. Otherwise he would only be a smoking pile of ash on the ground by now."

I countered the best I could, although Maebh did have a point, I had to explore the options, but this might not be as simple as I had hoped. An exorcism or equivalent would be possible and John would just be normal again.

"And he hasn't shown signs of conscious control at all?" Maebh asked, I could tell she was also reviewing the evidence that we had discussed and it wasn't looking good for her argument.

"No he hasn't, all the times things settled down were when he was back in control of his emotions. This would have been a restricting feature to a possessing force that would have been trying to exploit this emotional resonance.

Although that is assuming it was only a partial possession and he was still in conflict for control. I didn't get any clues that he was actively fighting anything and he was still self aware. But I think we can categorically say none of the magic he performed was the result of a conscious decision." Maebh nodded sadly to this, it seemed to all be stacking up neatly so I continued.

"And what about the visualisation of the problem and the river tide swallowing him up before he vanished? The transition into the wild version would make me think that his mind was being changed by something other than his own motivation. It was not a natural progression within the 'construct' that he had built from his own experiences. My eviction from it may have been down to my presence being viewed as a danger." I was growing more convinced as we reviewed the information.

"But hang on, you planted those ideas there before you put him into the trance." Maebh pointed out. "While it was John's consciousness and projection, you had already been speaking to him for a while beforehand about his problem, so it is not surprising that some the images he formed were influenced along the same lines of how you had explained things to him.

It was all in line with the wider concepts you had set out to him, and the eviction could have been a side effect of the shift in his own mind."

Maebh concluded by taking another sip of her coffee and watching me over the rim of the mug.

I stopped. That aspect hadn't occurred to me. How much of this might I have planted in his head, or even could have been drawn from other sources such as fiction rather than being representations of the actual forces? I really couldn't tell.

Had I fallen into the trap of taking things more at face value than they warranted? Magic and psychology are both equally treacherous when it comes to such things. Their greatest strength is simultaneously their great weakness, they are both very malleable.

"Do you think it was possible that my perception of that avatar was just my own interpretation?" Maebh inclined her head a little and then carried on with her point.

"We both know how subjective these things can be. I appreciate that you don't think he is just a rogue magic user, but I also don't see how the evidence entirely stacks up to prove your position either."

"But what about his role in Beltane?" I asked seeing if there was anything else that reinforced my position. "The green aspect. Why else has it taken these forms?"

As the words left my mouth I could feel the response growing behind my own lips. "As those were the ideas to which he had been most recently exposed...." I ended my own response in a groan. It is frustrating when you are able to see so many angles to something that the concept of a 'simple' truth is impossible to establish.

"Yes, so the magic would just take the most direct route and manifest in line with what he had been told about Beltane, and the Green Man." Maebh finished for me.

"Okay. Enough of the debate. I am willing to go forward with an open mind on what is actually happening." I took my cup over to the sink. "Irrespective of what is the underlying cause of these problems, what we need to do now is find John again and see what can be done!"

I looked over my shoulder and Maebh nodded and joined me at the sink. I felt her place her hand on my arm and give a small reassuring squeeze. Whatever happened next, and whatever we learnt about why it was happening, we were agreed we would face it together.

John

"So, an Angel, and a Devil..." talking to them seemed more sane than ignoring them, and would have felt impolite. Regardless of how weird the concept was. "And what is this laptop doing here?"

"I am here to guide you." the angel informed me continuing to use a tone of condescension. The angel sounded less irritated, but was shooting occasional disapproving glances at the devil.

"No. Angel here is going to try and stifle all the fun, and I am here to see that this doesn't happen! Now run along and see if you can get online, there are a few sites I could recommend to keep you busy, while I have a word with my colleague here." The devil started hefting its pitchfork as if contemplating having a quick stab, or testing out its aerodynamic properties.

"I think not." I said pretty certain that leaving them alone would not be wise. So far the angel had offered guidance, even if I wasn't sure it would be good, it was better than nothing. I pushed the power button again, hoping that a bit of persuasion would get things moving. This time it whirred into life. I was glad of the progress, even if it came with bitter memories. Whatever my feelings about it in the past, it was now my only clue.

The corporate logo based desktop appeared. My previous attempts to change it to anything else at all had been thwarted by IT who had locked all the settings down so that it remained the corporate standard. There was no room for personalisation.

"Hey, this is good. It normally took a lot longer to get going. I think it was nearly up to ten minutes of warming up by the time I handed it back to them. This has to be a fantasy, the brick would never be upgraded otherwise." I tried to include the angel and devil in case they gave me more clues.

"That is no surprise, you worked for a bunch of cheapskates – that piece of old rubbish is barely better than a typewriter." The devil interjected sarcastically poking the pitchfork towards the screen. I looked more closely at the desktop. While the logo was there, none of the icons I was used to seeing were there. Even the start menu was missing. All that I could see was a single PowerPoint presentation file called: 'John - Read Me'.

That seemed self-explanatory so I clicked on it to get it open. It opened straight into slideshow mode, and began to run itself. The title came up in two parts as a fly-in animation: 'All Work and No Play' which was swiftly followed by 'Makes John a BAD FRIEND'.

Whoever had put this together had gone all out on the special effects. I had reluctantly mastered the basics, but this was a little bit silly. There didn't seem to be any way to stop it, so I settled myself down more comfortably on the grass and watched it unfold.

Section by section, I was finding myself being deconstructed and dissected. It was not a kind critique, even my awful ex-Boss's evaluations had been kinder than this.

There were even charts, I felt those were much harsher than they needed to be. They were mostly showing how unreliable I had been in my social life. The ratio of promises made versus those kept was one I felt ashamed about.

It was made worse by the fact that they had even included a standard deviation model to show how I ranked against circumstantial breaches. Statistics can often be lies, but these were pretty damning as they were entirely true.

As it progressed there were even embedded video clips, showing a montage of the friends I had stood up for dinner or the movies. It even added analysis indicating the emotional fallout for my friends caused by the broken appointments. The final section analysed my work, how much time I had spent doing it, and how my boss had reacted. Normally fairly dismissively or apathetically. The page headed 'Conclusion' was quite simple. It read 'You wasted your time doing a job you hated and for which you got no recognition even when you went above and beyond. Your friendships were worth more.'

"But what is the point of this? I had to work, didn't I?" I turned to the angel and devil, there wasn't one particular thing that I had done was that bad. So how could it be shown that way? Despite what I was saying I could feel my stomach churn with the guilt that I had ignored. I had felt bad about letting people down, but there had always been a reason. "That was just putting a cruel spin on what happened. I'm not a bad person." I tried getting them to agree with me, help me feel less bad. It was the devil who spoke first.

"You should have blown off work more, that all just looked really dull. You weren't even enjoying it! And still you messed up despite it not making you happy. Are you some sort of idiot?"

I took a swipe at him, as the insult struck home. I felt like I had been a prick, that hurt. He ducked behind the angel who tried calming me down.

"Now, now. You need to realise what happened. Can't you see? There are limits to everything and what you did was place your obligations out of perspective. You gave more than you should have done to that one bit of your life, and sacrificed the rest. And to make matters worse, it wasn't even what you really wanted."

I made a half-hearted move to try and swat the angel but my anger was dying down again. It was true, I didn't want it to be, but I remembered again how it felt.

"But why does it matter how much I worked. Those were just a series of isolated incidents." I tried to convince myself that I hadn't done anything wrong. It wasn't working very well.

"Not everything is decided by grand actions. You took thousands of decisions, again and again. You made promises that you could have kept. You never really tried to make up for the mistakes that you made. The apologies were not very convincing as you didn't change anything."

The angel continued to be reasonable at me, which only served to make me feel more depressed. I sank down onto my folded arms, letting the truth sink in.

"You have a choice to make every day. Every time you are in a situation you have the power to choose, and looking back over that period of your life every time you seem to have made the bad choice.

You let down people who cared about you. A journey of a thousand miles may begin with a single step, but you have taken so many of those steps that you are more than halfway there."

The devil obviously feeling left out chimed in with "yeah, more than halfway to being a total arsehole! You should have had more fun. You didn't tell your boss where to stick his crappy job. That is what you did wrong! That was all far too boring."

"No," the angel began heatedly "That is not what he should have done. What he needed was to have better balance in his life." Then, to my surprise, the two of them began to scuffle with each other, arguing over whether it was fun or balance that was more important.

I watched them for a bit, and I felt the truth of what they were arguing about become more real for me. It made me realise that while they didn't agree with how I should have done it, I could still learn from what I did wrong. It was about having more fun, but it was also about keeping things better balanced as well. I had just been ignoring that part of myself.

The angel was right. I had let 'this time' become 'every time' and while I had apologised if I saw someone was upset, I never did anything to make it up to them.

The realisation started to bring the guilt from my stomach into a tightness in the chest, as I felt the grief that I had ignored over my lost friendships come bubbling to the surface.

My move to Edinburgh had only been so easy on a social level as I had by that point sacrificed pretty much all of my social life. If I hadn't stopped, I would have been even more isolated; I was lucky that Edinburgh had changed that. I was just going to have to be careful that I didn't let it happen again. I decided that the fight had gone on long enough so I reached out and grabbed one in each hand. Releasing them, they floated apart a bit.

"You are both right." They started dusting themselves off and casting evil glares at the other one. The harp and the pitchfork had both seen better days and were quickly dropped in a mangled heap next to the now dark laptop. The angel's halo was also a bit more wobbly, as were the devil's horns. With the loss of the props and the wobbly nature of their head gear, they were reminding me of something else but I couldn't work out what. One thing I was sure about was that they looked like they were going to carry on fighting.

"Now I want you two to make up, and promise to help me continue to sort this out, so that we can get out of this situation and on with whatever it is that we should be getting on with."

I stared them down, one at a time. Eventually I got reluctant nods from both of them which reassured me. The devil seemed the most reluctant. I turned back to look at the pool and it was now a little shallower than it had been before. It wasn't much, but there were a few extra inches of drowned grass at the edge, and the top of the mud wall showed a bit more clearly.

Green-John

I flowed into my body. Every cell alive.

It felt good.
I slowly reached out from my body.

The fabric of the shirt felt unnatural on my skin so I shrugged it off. Small static discharges crackled as I let it fall.

I opened my eyes to the dimness of the room.
It was so bland, so unstimulating.
This would never do.

I gestured and the barriers over the windows disappeared. The light streamed in.

It still didn't feel right. Everything was too close, too dark, to confining.

I reached down, to the heart of myself. Deeper down into the world, and called forth growth.

Beneath my feet the grasses and mosses began to sprout and spread across the floor. As I brushed the door frame, the wood remembered itself and became the tree it always was inside.

As I wandered the rooms I wanted more, more light, more life. The refuge I was using became better. Alive. The barrier to the sun above my growing friends was a problem so I willed it away. Stones became soil. The rafters becoming more trees.

A breeze stirred through my home. The fresh scents of the forest comforting me.

Something was different. I couldn't define it. My name was gone, but that was fine.

I was content being myself. For now I needed no name.

I reached deeper and called forth more life. As I reached for the earth I felt the sleeping minds that were nearby. Even those awake to the world were asleep to themselves. This was fun.

I visited each mind and stirred it. The urges that were withheld, ignored, forgotten. I opened their eyes for them. Freshened their senses. Helped them release the bonds that held them back.

Those fools in love I felt their passions rise and echo my joy in the world. Another echo called to me. A suppressed urge was there too, within this body. A yearning that was denied.

That would never do.

As I sought the answer to that question of desire, I felt her approach.

Still at a distance, but the strand of passion was there, and I could feel her grow nearer.

The flush of anticipation went through my body, soon.

Soon!

Maebh

It was a small victory that I could get Bridget to agree to disagree over the underlying cause of John's problem. The debate could have gone on for a while. But based on what she had told me and what I had seen, we were clear that there was a probable link between our experiences. It was definitely mystical and we had to act.

Once Bridget was back to full strength, we agreed to head over to John's flat. Since I had been there before, it wasn't a problem, I just hoped that this was where he had gone. I didn't tell Bridget how relieved I was that we didn't have to cross the Meadows again. Until whatever this was got resolved, I was going to be much more wary around plants.

"Can you feel that?" I asked, as we headed down Lothian Road. Despite the concrete and the tarmac I could feel the surging energy that was in the ground and the atmosphere.

"Yes. If I couldn't, we would have more things to worry about. And we still might," Bridget replied and gave a small nod towards a hanging basket outside a restaurant that we were passing. As I watched the flowers were slowly but visibly growing and a new blossom opened. I decided not to say anything so I just raised an eyebrow in response and we carried on.

"What do you think? It is already about 18 degrees would you say?" I felt the increasing temperature as a thickening texture in the air.

"Something like that, and it is probably going to get hotter. Did I tell you how I explained his condition to him? Reciprocal Seasonal Affective Disorder. I can only guess which set of emotions this is being fueled by. I think things have definitely gotten worse rather than better," Bridget responded, wiping her brow of the first beads of sweat.

"I think you are right, this is a bit too warm for this early in the day. Even in July. This is Scotland not Spain." I also wiped my face. The slight hints of breeze only teased at giving relief rather than actually helping. There were also worrying hints of spice and flowers that didn't seem to have any physical cause.

"It's all a bit quiet even for a Saturday morning. We've seen what, two cars? That isn't normal." I kept my voice down as we were passing the only other people we had seen, a couple of young women wearing as little as they could get away with. Not far behind them was an older man who must have been sweltering in his three-piece suit and hat. I cast Bridget a quizzical look, she waited until they were safely out of earshot before replying.

"Standards my dear. That gentleman wouldn't consider the hot weather as a good enough reason not to be as well-turned out as possible. It would be letting the side down or something like that? Although I suspect he is going to regret this later today; this a bit beyond what he would have been expecting. I agree, as well, it is far too quiet." I just nodded to that, we all know someone who would stick to the formalities over convenience. As we got to the other side of the Dean Bridge, the temperature increased rapidly, nearing tropical levels.

"Bugger, you were right." Bridget suddenly exclaimed. I halted in surprise, and she stopped with me.

"What?" I was worried.

"Look." She indicated towards the nearest garden. "Those plants, they are watching us. They feel 'expectant' I can't describe it any other way. It is downright unnerving. I can feel them watching us. I think if I shouted 'boo' they might jump back!" I just nodded again. I didn't trust myself to speak right now. It was very true and felt a lot stronger than it had on the Meadows. We were obviously getting closer to the centre of the disturbance. I wasn't sure it could get much worse.

As we turned the corner it got worse. The air felt thicker, and the temperature increased. I was dripping with sweat. Even the little teasing breaths of wind had now stopped, which made the movement of the trees I saw out of the corner of my eye even more disconcerting.

The atmosphere was strange, it was making me feel lethargic but was also bringing back other memories of hot days and nights. I looked up as we neared the flat and stopped again, unable to suppress a small noise of surprise. Bridget stopped too, and to my irritation didn't sound surprised.

"Hmm," Bridget responded. "I think I might have been able to find the place without you telling me which flat it is."

The entire tenement block was now a profusion of greenery. There even seemed to be trees growing out of the top floor. The ivy which sometimes added a hint of green to the normal stone tones of the buildings was now entirely covering the lower levels of the building.

The small sections of what were laughably called front gardens had now become alive with plants. Even the pavement immediately in front of the door was starting to buckle and crack with the roots and plants that had forced their way through.

"Do you hear that?" I asked Bridget, putting my finger on the other worrying element to all this.

"You mean that total lack of noise?" Bridget responded, her tone conveying her dissatisfaction with how quickly this had gone so very very wrong. "Not a bird, not an insect. I think they are avoiding it as it is all just a bit too unnatural. They might be the wiser ones."

"Can you make anything out? All I am getting from this is the overwhelming desire to put down roots and put forth some fruit." I wafted my hand around trying to cool myself off a little.

"I am starting to get something. But it is a bit messy. Try and pull back your focus a little. Think of it like an impressionist painting. If you look too closely, all you get is blobs of colour. You are right, the urges are definitely focusing on growth and fertility, but there is a little bit more going on." Bridget was also wiping the sweat from her face. As I pulled back the focus of my perception as she had suggested, it all came into focus. I shivered, the sweat suddenly feeling cold.

"Bloody hell, that is all turned up to 11 in there. What are we going to do? It is looking a bit dangerous." I looked at Bridget, and the fixed line of her jaw made me wish I hadn't asked. "Maybe I should go and buy a machete? Or would a flamethrower be better?"

"No, I don't think so. This isn't going to respond well to that." Bridget paused and turned to look at me. Her smile small, tight and a bit scary. "I am a bit surprised, you are wanting to go all Rambo on these plants."

"Well, you weren't the one who had been grappled by the grass on the Meadows, and it is all just starting to creep me out a bit more. Do you remember that film "Day of the Triffids"? My brother let me watch it when I was far too young. It took me ages to convince myself that murderous plants felt like a ridiculous idea. Right now, I am not sure, and don't want to take any chances." I shivered again at the memory.

"Okay, that makes sense. However there's not enough time. If it's this bad now, by the time you get back, it could be a thousand times worse." Bridget responded. "You stay here and see what you can do about dissipating some of the worst of it, or at least not letting it spread until I can get through to him." Bridget was sizing up the situation and was about to just walk right into it. I grabbed her arm.

"Are you sure? Is this we best way to handle it? We could see if we can find anyone else? This will be bringing other witches out of the woodwork I am sure. We could get more help." I tried to reason with her but I could tell she wasn't listening.

"I'm sorry but I have to do this. This is at least partially my mess. I have to go in there to find out what state my 'patient' is in and that is non-negotiable. I need you to try and siphon off the energy to stop it getting worse. Do you think you can do that?" Bridget was barely looking at me. The pull of the situation was taking all her attention.

"Okay. But be quick." I nodded and let go of her arm. She made her way into the greenery. The path was still relatively clear.

Watching her go, I was struck by the mixed-up parallels to Sleeping Beauty, as Bridget fought her way into the plants that had overgrown the 'castle'. She didn't acknowledge my final comment, but given that I think she was trying to ensure that there were no additional magical surprises lurking in the way, that was sensible. I watched her get a bit further in and swore when I saw it was beginning to close up behind her.

There was no way she was going to be able to back down from this, even if she did change her mind.

I walked back a short distance. Trying to gauge what would be safe so I wasn't taken by surprise. None of it felt that safe, so I settled down on the side of the pavement across the road from the tenement.

I tried to not let self-doubt get in my way. When it comes to magic I prefer reading the strands of energy rather than tugging on them. Bridget is way more comfortable doing that, she just stomps in and makes stuff happen.

I hadn't really been joking about the machete, but she was right, we didn't have time for that right now. I felt like a pastry chef being asked to make sushi. Nothing for it. I was going to do the best that I could. Bridget needed this help. I dove into the energies and pulled.

Bridget

Maebh's attempts to reason with me were understandable, but when I saw the result of my previous failure, I didn't feel able to wait. I could feel a strong pull. He was in there. Waiting for me. I was partly responsible for this mess, and it was obviously getting worse. We really didn't have time to wait. My patient was still in need of help and whether he was possessed or was a newly awakened magic user of ridiculous power, this situation was out of hand and it had to be resolved.

I could feel the pull of the magic as I walked forward into the narrow pathway between the greenery. The attraction to power is an innate part of witchcraft, or it was for me. I knew that Maebh felt differently, but there was always strand of a desire for control that comes with magic users. Something within us that sought it out.

I did my best to hold myself back from allowing the power to flow through me. It was both my strength but right now was also a new risk. I didn't know how deeply he was gone into the power. I took a moment to pause, it was feeling far too easy, I looked back and regretted it. The lesson from the classics was one I should have listened to, the sight of the path disappearing behind me.

The still moving wall of thorns and roses entwining made me briefly regret my earlier confidence. However, I was now without any other choice, so I carried onwards into the heart of the forest.

I could barely tell when I had crossed the threshold of the door, as it had become a pair of saplings, it was just the change in the quality of light that let me know I was inside. I checked and the path to the back green was also cut off by thorns and a final backwards glance confirmed for me that the only way really was up. I let myself hum the tune that went with that thought, but I stopped quickly as it sounded far too nervous and that made me feel more uncomfortable. The silence was better. It let me focus on my feelings.

As I climbed the stairs, the maelstrom of magic continued around me, and the heat strengthened. I paused to loosen my clothing to try and make it feel less oppressive. As I stopped, I realised it was less silent than I had previously thought. As I tuned my ears into the unexpected noise, I also opened myself up a little bit more to the quality of the magic to determine what was going on around me. The sensation of erotic stirrings, echoed the sounds I could now distinguish coming from the flats on this floor.

"I suppose that is why they haven't noticed anything," I muttered as I carried on upwards. The doors that I passed were all completely sealed off with ivy and thorns, so I knew I still had to climb some more.

The atmosphere was starting to have an effect me. My own feelings of desire began to surface, memories of flirtations and other exploits came back to me. John's face smiling over dinner came back to me as well. I did my best to redirect these feelings. Allowing them to dissipate into the magic around me.

It was akin to Judo, using the momentum to keep yourself from being overwhelmed. However, the effort of the redirection was increasing my temperature further. I was running out of options for loosening my clothing as I wasn't willing to face up to whatever was happening up there in just my bra.

The heat and the exertion of the climb started sapping my energy. I allowed my hand to push myself on by touching the railings, covered in ivy, the jolt of sensation that came with it nearly knocked me over. The memories that I had been only partly experiencing suddenly became full sensory replays. I pulled my hand away as if I had been burnt and cradled it against my body. Taking a moment to gather myself, I needed to brace myself for this. It felt something of an understatement to say it was going to be very difficult.

As I reached the top floor, the surface under my feet changed from the worn stone of the stair to a light springy moss. It was completely covering the floor. It was obvious where I had to go, the only path lead through what I guessed had once been a door but was now a couple of saplings framing the entrance to a forest glade.

As I crossed the ruined threshold, the temperature dropped from the Saharan extreme down to that of a very pleasant summer's day and a soft breeze began to play across my skin. Looking up, I could tell from the way that sunshine was dappling through the leaves that it was unlikely that there was still a roof up there. If we were still actually in the tenement anymore. I couldn't be sure, the place was so saturated with magic that we could have been anywhere.

"I like what you've done with the place." I said to no-one in particular, hoping that John would respond and it would not be as bad as it looked. The silence began to unnerve me a little. "Green is very in this season, I hear." I continued to look around but only managed a half-hearted smile at my own joke. While the temperature had dropped, the magic in the atmosphere was nearly overwhelming,.

"I'm glad you like it." A voice said gently just by my ear.

The surprise of him being there that close to me made me freeze. I hadn't seen or sensed anyone along the way, but given the overload that wasn't surprising. My instincts to avoid detection by stopping movement were sadly wrong in this context. The next thing, I was aware of a warm hand on my shoulder, that traced a path down my arm. Even through the fabric of my shirt my skin felt cool in comparison to the heat that was emanating from him. I carefully turned around to face him. Steeling myself to face up to whatever had happened to him.

I quickly assessed him, using the skills normally there for triage of health issues. This time to work out what the magical impact had been from my first intervention. It was obviously still John, but the skin tone had altered from his British pallor to a ruddier, maybe just more tanned complexion.

Looking closely it seemed to me that there was a slight change to the line of the jaw, it looked firmer. It could have just been more tense than normal. The thing that worried me most were his eyes.

They were no longer blue.

They had changed to a deep brown with fleck of green and gold. I found myself staring deeply into them trying to read what was going on beneath the surface. It was captivating; I suddenly became aware of the truth that came from the old cliché, I felt I was falling into them. He was open to me and I was voluntarily going deeper.

I felt myself letting go of my control, allowing my attraction both to the man I had eaten dinner with the previous night and the raw power that was emanating from the figure before me overwhelm my self-control. I struggled with that. Suppressing my own desires.

The attraction that I felt was unprofessional. This was not the right time. This was the wrong place. He was not the right person. He was still my patient. He wasn't himself. This was dangerous. Exciting but dangerous.

He stood there smiling at me. His shirt hanging open a little. I felt my eyes drawn down by my curiosity to appreciate the hint of chest that was on display. I controlled myself to not allow them to drift further.

Returning to his face, I found the smile was broader. My body began to rebel against the self-imposed limits that I had established. I listened to my body. He was there, open, inviting.

I stopped resisting.

I tilted my head. Took a step forward. Leant in a little. I kissed him. He kissed back.

The surge I felt this time was different from the one in cafe. It was far stronger, but also more subtle. It was not the force of a hurricane knocking me from my feet but a storm surge of water, lifting me but holding me safe in its power. It was a combination of my own power and that outside of me, working in harmony.

His heat, my coolness, my senses could no longer distinguish between them. All I felt was my body ache for closer contact, for inclusion in what I was feeling around me. Allowing my own passions free rein was liberating. I normally kept them safely locked away until it was appropriate. I connected to the call and response of attraction. My desire rose in response to the situation. I had a moment of choice. I could slam down my own feelings or to allow them to continue to flow freely. I hesitated. He broke away from the kiss and looked at me. His eyes searching mine. Still inviting, but not demanding. I grabbed his face and pulled it back towards mine and kissed him again.

The renewed flow of energy between us, both his into me and mine into him, freed me. The moment was all. My previously denied pleasure became all. He was open to me and we merged. Our bodies became the entire world.

John

"Bridget?" I stopped, looking up from where I had gone back to, trying to clear the mud. I thought I had heard her, or felt her nearby somehow. There was no sign. The feeling that she was with me lingered, but she didn't respond and I couldn't see her anywhere. I rinsed my face and hands off. I moved a bit further out of the pool and called again, but there was no sign. I put it down to wishful thinking and turned back to the task at hand. I wasn't sure how much time had passed but I was missing her, and not just as a sanity check against my little companions.

The devil and the angel had quickly gotten bored after the laptop had died again, and I went back to digging into the mud. They had begun squabbling over the broken harp and pitchfork and doing their best to try and force them to work again. The angel was having it a little worse as the halo was now not as secure in its hovering position and kept slipping into jaunty angles or falling off completely. They had each started trying to lecture me on their interpretation of what had happened; neither was particularly flattering so I decided it was best if I return to digging through the mud.

They left me alone as long as I was in the water working on trying to clear the blockage. I watched them for a little bit after I thought I had felt Bridget and they didn't seem to be doing particularly well.

The angel appeared to be trying to pray and wasn't making much progress, being distracted by the halo slipping.

The devil on the other hand was wandering in small circles jabbing the grass with the broken remains of his pitchfork, when he wasn't trying to make eye contact with the angel and smirk about his slipping halo. The fact that these supernatural creatures also seemed to be having their own crisis of identity amused me, it made me feel less alone. Misery loves company.

I went back to the mud before they noticed me watching them. I hadn't found anything since the laptop, but it felt good to be trying. It was really quite meditative and it was giving me time to think about what I had seen before. It was helping me see my failures from a slight distance. It had felt harsh at the time but there was something in what the presentation had said. Other memories surfaced briefly and I thought about them differently, and it helped me realise how I needed to be different. How to make wiser choices. Sometimes less selfish, sometimes more selfish, but all to reflect what I actually wanted to do and not what I thought I was supposed to do.

I pushed my hands deeper; it still was very giving when I pushed, but was difficult to find anything in there, so I just had to keep searching. My fingers brushed something. It was a round edge. Smooth. I found it difficult to get a good grip, but I pushed my arm deeper and found a way to get my fingers around the thin line that my fingertips were defining as I probed. I had to bring my head down to the level of the water, and brought my other arm in from a different angle to ensure I didn't lose it.

I grasped it tightly and pulled. It was a disc, less than a foot across, but completely covered in mud and grime.

I put it under the water and moved it around to try and wash off the build up, and had to rub at it quite hard to begin to remove the thick layer of dirt. It had a familiar feel, and quite quickly with my rubbing I was able to see what it was. It was a frisbee. Not just any frisbee, but my old frisbee. The one I had picked up in a charity shop on the corner of the street by my hall of residence. Back in first year at University. It was easy to recognise. It was frankly hideous. The colour had been a lurid day-glo purple and I had never seen another one like it since. I had thought it was hideous at the time as well, but I wanted a frisbee.

"Bloody hell, that is awful." The devil was now standing at the edge of the water watching me. "Is that another piece of crap from your past? Just throw it away."

"No, don't listen to him…" the angel started. "Good grief, that is awful." The angel's reaction to the frisbee made me smile as the tone became more genuine rather than just sounding trite.

"I like it." I lied. I remembered similar conversations with people when I first bought it. "Okay, maybe it is just a horrified fascination." It felt odd trying to lie to them so I clarified.

"Well, at least it would be easy to find again. I am certain nothing in nature is that particular shade of purple." The angel tried to sound positive, possibly making up for the previous comment.

"I can think of a few unnatural things that colour." The devil waggled his eyebrows at me. I ignored him but continued back to the edge of the water. I wanted to get out of the water to think about what this was supposed to represent.

"I can't remember what it used to say." I traced the contrasting lime green pattern that was now too faded to make out any details. "I used to have to hide this when I had a bad hangover, but that doesn't feel like an important lesson from my past."

I sat down on the grass between them again. Trying to see what memories it would bring up.

"It was a good frisbee, we used it a lot towards the end of first year." I lay down on my discarded shirt and turned it over in my hands.

"I still think you should just chuck it away. It is just a bit of tat." I went to swat him with the frisbee as I could tell he was in no mood to actually be helpful.

"If you can't help me, just bugger off." I resisted the urge to throw the frisbee at him as he glowered at me after jumping back out of the way.

"It is not our job to help you exactly. Just to be here while you uncover your problems. It is my role to guide you into understanding," the angel chimed in, "and help you resist temptation," it added smugly, looking at the devil.

"Yeah, whatever," the devil responded.

I flipped onto my back and held the frisbee over my head. I was immediately dry and comfortable again. The temptation to close my eyes for a nap surfaced but I pushed it away, I had to work this out first. I sat up again turning it around and over in my hands.

"What can I do with this?" I asked not really expecting much help. "It's not like the laptop. I can't get it to tell me anything."

"Nothing, it's not like a magic sword, or something." the devil chimed in.

"What does it mean to you? Do you feel anything?" the angel asked trying to sound more serious, but looking doubtful.

"All I can feel is scuffed plastic. It was just a cheap toy that I bought to make the trips to the park a bit more entertaining. We had a lot more time back then. It was in the run up to the first year exams. They hadn't been serious enough to stop us going to the park when the weather was good." It all started coming back to me. I smiled at the thought. We had on occasion taken our books and notes as well, but mostly it had been about beer and frisbee.

"Now that sounds much better, maybe you should focus on having fun. Much better than dusty old books!" The devil suggested.

"No, it sounds like there might be a lesson about focus and commitment. Maybe self discipline?" The angel responded, sounding very put out that the devil was still trying to get this to just be about fun.

"I can't remember the last time I saw this, it must have disappeared in one of my previous flat moves. Years ago." I now couldn't take my eyes off it, there was something about it that I should remember, but nothing was coming to mind.

"You need to meditate on its message, seek the truth within." The angel held forth, briefly patting my knee. Giving me exactly the trite sort of answer I expected.

"Nah, you need to get rid of this old piece of junk and stop listening to this naff wannabe." The devil also now approached and tentatively poked my other knee to underline his point.

"Do you have anything useful to suggest? The rubbish about focus and commitment isn't ringing any bells. And please don't try and make this moral. If your plan is to irritate me into spiritual enlightenment, I would rather give it a miss. And you, little devil, are really quite rubbish at leading me into temptation. I really don't know why I got the pair of you. I've not been to church since I was able to just say 'no' and decide that a lie-in and football were better. However, you are all that I've got right now. So give it another go."

They both looked a little put out by what I said, but I had gone beyond caring. I just kept on playing with the frisbee hoping that like some magical puzzle box just flipping it over and over would make it tell me what I was supposed to know. The silence grew strained. Out of the corner of my eye I could see the angel struggling to decide what to do.

"You're breaking the rules." The angel blurted out suddenly. "This shouldn't be happening. You aren't playing things safely." This didn't make much sense, but seemed important.

"Woohoo, now you are breaking them too!" the devil added. "Exactly why this is so much FUN! But don't worry about this ninny. You can carry on having fun and that is all fine with me. So just forget about this stuff and stop muckraking."

"No. It really can't go on. It isn't safe." The angel stepped closer and rested a small hand on my wrist; the hand was quite cool. I allowed my frisbee fiddling to stop as I looked down at it.

"Safe, schmafe. Don't listen to that nonsense, of course it can," the devil added laying a small, and much warmer, hand on my other wrist. As that happened I felt a moment of connection between us and there was the sound of a bell chiming. The frisbee in my hands suddenly jerked and felt warm. We all looked down at it.

It was upside down, presenting a small shallow bowl. The surface went black and gave the impression of swirling movement. My hands were locked and I was unable to move.

My attention was pulled deeper into the frisbee and the scene developing in my lap. It seems my companions were equally drawn as I could see them in my peripheral vision leaning in to get a better view.

Within the moving darkness, a small dot of light appeared. It reminded me of how my grandmother's old television had come to life, on those occasions when we visited her and I was allowed to turn it on. It gradually grew in detail, slowly swelling into colour and detail.

It was the park where we had used to play with the frisbee.

It looked like any day. Fred, Joe and I came into the field of vision. We were just about to start playing. I couldn't hear but I could tell from the way we were shoving each other that we were having the normal banter, the casual insulting of your friends as a sign of affection.

The memory made me smile.

I realised it had been years since I spoke to either of them. I missed that. It could have been any day, but there was something about the scene below that began to bring about specific feelings. I felt sad, unhappy. That didn't fit, we had always had such a great time, there would be no reason for me to think that this was a bad memory. What was it about this day?

I let myself feel it, letting the sadness out. Trying to remember what had been the cause.

As I did so, the perspective shifted and it was now all coming from my point of view. I was both there feeling how happy I was, enjoying the teasing, running around and there, feeling the sadness that this memory brought with it.

It still didn't make any sense.

The game was going well. Fred threw to me again, but it was too high. The trajectory wasn't too bad to work out. I could definitely get it. Fred's throw seemed to presume I was much further away, so I began to gently jog backwards. My eyes fixed on the slowly spinning disc. Making sure that it was still doing what I thought it was going to do. The details behind it were very clear. The bright blue sky, a small fluffy cloud, the bird - all of them giving a backdrop to the key piece of information. The purple frisbee. My arm coming into view to snatch it from the air.

Just as my hand closed on it everything went wrong.

My smooth backwards jog became a tumble. Something was under my legs and I was spinning through the air. After a brief jumble of confused bits of information I came to a halt. Flat on my back. Still clutching my frisbee.

The noise of unhappy people quickly became very clear. The picnic that had broken my fall was definitely not going to be in a good state. I could feel my face flushing with shame again. The breath had been knocked out of me so I had to lie still for a bit longer. The legs and far off faces of the people whose lunch I had ruined framed my view of the still blue sky. Watching them wipe food and drink from their clothes. I was about to shut my eyes and wish myself out of existence.

Just as I was about to, a new face came into view. Upside down from my perspective.

The eyes caught my attention as they were a startling brown, with small flecks of gold. Her dark lips contrasting with the soft brown of her skin. She had a gentle smile.

"Thank you so much for dropping in. But you seem to be in my tzatziki. Are you okay?" The voice was soft and managed to combine both concern and amusement. The moment froze for me.

I could feel again how my heart rate which had started to slow down again after my fall began to race again when she spoke to me. I had heard of the cliche of love at first sight, but this made me a believer. Sadly, I also became aware that I was looking stupid and clumsy and I just felt too humiliated.

The vision switched to an external view again. I could see my face was red. I just jumped up and apologised and ran away. Clutching my frisbee. I could feel again the hurt that I had forgotten about. My anger at my own stupidity. Still inside me, but buried away. The heat of the shame flushed my face again.

It all came back.

Joe and Fred helped me gather our stuff up and gave the combination of support and mockery that was the centre of our friendship. Making a joke of pain helped to forget how much it had hurt.

As we walked away from the scene of my disgrace, the vision faded back to black, and then back to the purple of the frisbee.

I no longer cared. I now remembered why it was an important thing. For all it was cheap and nasty plastic, it had been there at an embarrassing moment of my life and I had forgotten.

I could feel my eyes burning, but I wasn't able to cry. The shame stopped me.

"Wow, she was Hot!" The devil exclaimed, breaking the tension of the moment. "Why did you run away? She seemed to be into you even after you had made such a prat of yourself!"

"What is this all about?" I tried to get them to talk so I didn't have to think about what I had just been reminded about. "It was embarrassing, but it was years ago."

"What this is about, young man, is that you were too proud to admit that you were imperfect and so ran away from something that could have been good for you, just as it started badly." The angel sounded genuinely sympathetic, but the words hurt. It was too true. I had forgotten it for a reason.

"Oh, wow – that is weird," the devil joined in; "We are nearly in agreement, what I think is that he was too chicken to take a risk. She was a hottie, you could have been in there and you ran off."

I looked at both of them; they suddenly seemed uncomfortable with the fact that they were in agreement and weren't certain what to do next if they weren't arguing.

I tried to hold back the tears, but it didn't work. I started sobbing, allowing myself to feel the regret over what I had left behind. The jokes at the time had helped numb it, but the pain was still underneath it all. Still fresh.

"I didn't even know her name, we barely spoke, why is that one encounter significant?"

I tried to rationalise the pain away. It was ridiculous.

"What does your heart tell you? Can you really say that this was insignificant? Do you really not see how quickly you fell in love." Through the tears I couldn't tell which avatar spoke, but was sure that as it hadn't been crude, it had to have been the angel.

"Love? How could it be love? But it was, wasn't it? I was in love. She was a total stranger but apparently that doesn't matter." allowing the truth of the words to take shape as I said them, it made me realise exactly what it was that I had turned away from.

"Whoever she was, I loved her." I was grateful that neither the angel or devil chose to speak, but let me carry on. "I was such an idiot, she didn't seem to mind, but I just couldn't bring myself to stay. I felt like such a … prat." The memory of the kindness of her smile made me cry harder.

I looked up at the angel and devil and they weren't even looking at me. As I watched there was a swirl of water in the pool and the level dropped by another couple of inches.

They glanced back at me, and then turned and walked away from each other.

I sat there and allowed myself to grieve properly for what I had missed out on, due to my own stubborn pride. The ability to accept love despite myself.

Bridget

I opened my eyes. I awoke and felt fully back in control. I felt good. It was unreal but gradually it came back to me. The memory was all there. I stretched a little feeling the gentle ache in my muscles as a reminder that I hadn't just imagined it all. It had been so good, but I began to feel conflicted. I had been selfish. I had given into my desires. Far too easily.

I was supposed to be helping him. I really hoped it hadn't made it worse. I wasn't sure exactly where we were anymore but I remember that we had moved. There had definitely been some flying, or so I thought. It was hard to separate the magical from the tactile in the past few hours. But it looked like we were in a different location, and the atmosphere had changed.

I now had to assess the situation. I was alone. My immediate view was limited. I was inside an odd shelter. It was probably best called a bower, having been made by small trees that seem to have grown woven together. Their leaves dappling the light that broke through to illuminate the floor. Whatever time it was, the sun was still strong.

I was pretty certain that it had only been a couple of hours. Gauging the light, this seemed about right. Underneath me was a comfortable mattress of moss, soft grasses and occasional flowers. As I ran my fingers across it, an intoxicating scent filled the air. It evoked some of the recent memories that I was still integrating. I felt myself blush a little.

I sat up to take in more of my environment and realised as the fabric moved strangely against my skin that I wasn't in my normal clothes. I stood up to get a better look. I was now wearing a beautiful gown that initially appeared to be of a deep green. As I moved it shimmered with different shades and tones. As I ran my hand over it I could feel it was like silk but changed colour as I touched it and intensified the feelings that went through to my skin.

"Definitely not polycotton." I muttered, enjoying the feeling. Controlling myself, I stopped stroking the fabric. I sat down again to think. As I did I started running my hand over the bedding, the tactile feedback felt good. I felt a slight resistance against my fingers, a snag. Curious, I twisted my fingers and pulled against it. With an inaudible snap they came free. Bringing them to my face, I found some hairs tangled in them. Looking closely, I realised that they were not mine. An idea came to me. To keep them safe, I pulled out a small handful of the bedding and wrapped it into a small bundle. I clutched it tightly in my fist.

I had wasted enough time. I guessed that John couldn't be too far away, but decided to not try and find him magically. Reaching out might leave me too open to my desires. This had definitely not been the plan, but worrying about that now wasn't going to help. I needed to come up with a better solution next time. My last gamble hadn't paid off. I headed out of the bower, praying to all the gods that we hadn't gone very far.

The midday sun briefly dazzled me as I left the shade. As my eyes adjusted, I breathed a sigh of relief. We were still in Edinburgh.

The bower was only a few metres from the edge of a cliff, and below me the city lay spread out across its multiple hills and glens. We were on Salisbury Crags. Below me, I surveyed the buildings; they seemed to be covered in a lot more ivy. And I was almost certain that the trees were looking taller than normal.

Looking closer, I realised that the Queen's Drive was completely hidden by grass and other plants. It seems some other changes had taken place. A soft breeze stirred my new dress and the fabric iridesced as it rippled. I started at a footfall behind me, but I didn't turn around.

"You get such a nice panorama from here, don't you think?" It was the voice of the being that looked like John. I realised now I couldn't treat him as if he were John. Not anymore. Now I was listening more closely, I realised there was a deeper resonance to the voice. I decided not to turn around. It was easier if I didn't look at him for the time being.

"Yes, you do, and so nice to have it without it being cluttered with tourists. It makes such a nice change."

I schooled my voice to sound light and pleasant. Doing my best to not give any sign of what I was feeling. I pushed down the growing anxiety I wouldn't be able to resist next time, I wouldn't be able to not want to.

I couldn't risk him touching me again. I turned and gave him a bright, but not entirely truthful smile. It softened with genuine feeling when I saw him.

He was now shirtless and I was struck by how remarkably attractive he was. My resolve wavered a little. This was going to be a dangerous dance, not just because of his power, but because of my own desire.

The fine torture of being torn between curiosity, attraction and fear. My acknowledgement of that internal battle made something click in my mind. It could be the key to the situation. With that knowledge, I felt calmer and more energised. I just needed to make an actual plan.

"So what now?" I asked keeping my tone light "I see you are making some changes down there. What's your plan?" I probed for more information hoping to buy myself a little extra time. Everything I had learned from John the previous day was potentially useless. I had to see what had changed. Could I get any new information to help me understand what had happened to him?

"Plan? I don't know. There is no plan. That sounds boring. There is just what is fun. I do so enjoy letting things happen. When I feel constrained, I stretch. When I have an itch, I scratch."

The John-shaped figure tilted his head as he responded, looking like a quizzical animal. A lazy hand reached up and rubbed itself across his bare chest and taut belly. I pulled my eyes away from following its path across his body.

"What do I call you?" I asked a little desperate to change the topic. I made the mental adjustment to treat him, and this situation, as a puzzle. Not as a man.

It helped to move away from the complications that I had previously distracted me. Given how I had gotten it wrong twice before, I definitely didn't want to jump to the wrong conclusions again. I had to assess what was happening carefully. He didn't respond. He continued to observe me, moving slowly around where I was standing. I felt like I was watching an animal stalking its prey.

"I don't think I can call you John anymore. While you look like him and maybe part of him is still in there, I believe there is something more going on. And it's not quite what I thought before either." I kept on talking at him. Testing him. Seeing how he was responding to my words.

"You are definitely connected to the Green Man. But I see now that you're not just an avatar. This isn't a possession. He isn't riding you against your will." He was restless. I was grateful he was still keeping his distance, but I couldn't tell for how long.

"Oh, you can call me John. If you want, it is just a label. I am as much John as I ever was." He responded slowly, the words pulled from him reluctantly. I kept observing his movements, the pace of the stalking was consistent.

But he was edging closer. Slowly. The hunter not wanting to startle its prey, but definitely getting ready to pounce. In the cafe he had seemed like an acrobat, now his movements were primal. It was just as graceful, but infinitely more dangerous.

"So that name serves as well as any. I am John. I am the part of him that rarely got to speak or act. I am the unvoiced cry, now heard. I am the restrained impulse, unleashed. I am all that he wishes when not turning against his own desires. I am the growth of desire and the rhythm in the blood. I am man and nature. All nature that seeks to expand beyond what it is now."

I could feel his emotions rising as he stated his nature. The energy radiating from him became stronger.

The allure of that power battered against my resolve to not give in to the temptation. I was relieved to feel that I was able to resist so far.

"Sorry, should I join you in a chorus of 'I am what I am'?" I edged further away from him trying to keep the right balance of being close enough to read him but not within reach if he decided to lunge forward. My heart rate increasing in response to the situation, my nerves making my initial response flippant.

"You definitely need some excuses in this case. You have gone too far! There are limits to these things. The balance is destroyed when one element subsumes another. You are neither man nor god. You are a broken soul buoyed up with magic and no good can come of this."

I went with the melodrama of the moment. It seemed appropriate to try and match his hyperbole.

"Oh, why say that? You are wrong. I am not broken. If anything, I am more whole than I had been before. How can you say that this is not good?

Can you not feel the sun on your face? Does the breeze in your hair not feel good? I know the heart beating in your chest echoes me. The good earth beneath your feet feels just as good to you. I can feel you as the waves to my moon and the moon to my waves. It is within our blood. How can you not see that all this is good? Isn't anything that leads us away from this bad? So why do you need to label things?"

He continued to slowly move around me. Side to side, always moving. Each turn bringing him inch by inch closer.

I glanced around. Realising that our gradual drift of pursuit and retreat had brought us closer to the edge of the crags. My inner voice was keeping me from falling under his influence through self-control and careful sarcasm. The thought 'but Grandmother what big teeth you have' very nearly slipped out as another flippant comment.

The pull of his power was growing. My options were getting more limited. His monologue was useful, but it still wasn't quite conclusive enough. I weighed up multiple potential reasons. Was this just insanity caused by magic, or was it an unusual form of possession, or was it a bit more complicated?

"I need to know, John. I might be a Witch but I am also a scientist. I am quite fond of labels. They are limited, but they do have their uses.

As a doctor, your doctor in fact, I have already given you a diagnosis, and I am sorry to say that the treatment isn't going to plan."

I deliberately used his name again to see if that would reverse or reduce the nature god rant. Trying to goad him to see if there was a spark of the original personality in there. Had it all been drowned out in the flow of power? I changed my approach again.

"It is one of my many foibles. I have a need to know. For me, knowledge is somewhat of a drug, I'm hooked. Like all addictions, it doesn't always make me happy, but they do say the first stage is accepting that you have a problem. What's your problem John? Can you tell me?" My challenge seemed to have struck home. He paused in his gradual approach. His similarity to a confused animal was growing stronger by the moment as he struggled with what seem to be alien concepts.

"I don't know why you keep on resisting me. I can feel your desire. You push it down deep inside. It calls to me. I am. You are. We could be together. We could be so much. It was fun. It is fun. Impulses are there for us to listen to them. Desire is there to be satisfied. Anything else is a denial of life. I know you can feel the tide of power. Ride it with me. Take my hand again. Come with me."

I could hear the promise in what he was saying. He was right, if I did take his hand we would be having fun. But I knew it wouldn't be right. He was almost pleading with me.

My refusal made no sense to him, and I could feel his confusion. That was another piece to the puzzle I filed away. His acceptance of the power, of the magic, was instinctual, very different from the man I met yesterday.

This was not an offer that John alone would have understood enough to make. Yet, this was an offer. It wasn't just blind force. The power unmitigated by awareness wouldn't have sought my agreement. That meant there was still humanity in there.

I don't believe that Cernunnos would have pleaded with me either. That spirit was old enough to understand the limitations of humanity. This was definitely an intricate and fascinating puzzle. The balance might be the key.

The factors seemed to include room for intent, the need for choice, the rawness of the power tearing through normal natural boundaries and limits. Maybe this problem was even more basically human than I had suspected?

"I'm sorry. You are right; I do have the desire to give in, but I have to resist. Fun it may be, but there are times and seasons and balances to these things. What I see here is not meant to be. This is just a bit wrong! I promise you that I will see you again. I promised you my help yesterday and I intend to keep my word. However right now, I need a bit of space."

As I made this final speech, I backed myself towards the very edge of the crags. The rough stone making it clear when I was at the brink. The conflict I had set up by refusing and challenging him was making him desperate.

The force had been increasing as we spoke, the emotional feedback creating a strong vortex in the energy. I had learnt enough for now and I needed to think more deeply about what to do next. I needed a new plan. Tapping into the magic that was flowing around me, and through me, I decided to make an exit. Without any fear, I stepped backwards. Off the crags.

I dropped a few feet until I opened up my connection to the magic and flew. It is not easy. But when you are able to make the right adjustments to yourself and the surrounding world you can make gravity temporarily optional. The myth of broomsticks was just a convention, it made it easier to shift the power around when you had another object to provide focus.

It was entirely unnecessary as you were changing your own nature to be less on the physical plane and instead it becomes possible to move within the flows of energy that you became one with. For a while. The magic comes from the person in this case, not the object.

"Maebh. I'm safe. I need you. Meet me back at my cottage." I cried out to her telepathically briefly splitting my focus to let her know what was happening. Pulling back my focus, I made my escape. It was risky and if he decided to pursue me it would be very dangerous, but I needed distance to think.

I normally would have tried to make myself unnoticed as well, but time and speed were of the essence. It was a different risk, but given the odd things that were going on, they hopefully wouldn't stop to comment on any reports of a woman flying down from Salisbury Crags.

This was a necessary tactical retreat. Descending from the cliff, I could see more clearly the influence of this unleashed power in the world below. There were very few people moving around. Even the magically unaware people could recognise when things weren't safe. The atmosphere was tense.

If this was happening, a lot it was getting more serious than just my promise to help John. If he wasn't stopped, we would be facing a world where one man had the power to make anyone embrace their desires regardless of consequences. Where you would have to keep him happy to secure good weather. It would be a return to the world of fairytales, and not the nice ones.

I checked and there was no sign of pursuit so I redirected some of the energy to conceal myself and descended further into the city centre. Discretion reasserting itself once the urgency had diminished.

As I landed, I paused to check that I still had the handful of moss from the bed. It might be the wedge that I needed to break the situation open. The oldest magics are often the most reliable.

I dispelled the illusion and hurried on home to my cottage. I hoped I had enough time to change before Maebh got here. I didn't want her to know how far things had gone. The dress would only lead to questions I didn't want to answer right now. But I also hoped she wouldn't be long as I would need her to help me if the ghost of a plan that I had started forming was going to be able to work.

Green-John

It was a beautiful day. The energy was flowing much more freely.

She had arrived. We had fun.
I felt satisfied. I left her to rest.

I was strolling around enjoying the feeling of the fresh air on my skin and the ground beneath my feet. I had fended people away from here. I wanted to be alone with her.

I sensed her start to move around. I moved to a spot where I could watch her.

She was beautiful. I went to join her, hoping for a new embrace.

For some more fun.

She was wary, she was hiding it, but I could tell. Her desire for me was still there, but it was harder for me to reach. I felt she was trying to get away from me. I began to follow her carefully.

She began asking questions. So many questions. So many dull, dull answers. I did my best to give her the answers. It might bring her back from the distance she had created between us.

It wasn't working. I could feel her move further away inside herself. But she was still reaching out to me. She felt the pull as well as I did.

It was very confusing. Why would she want to refuse? There was so much joy in saying yes. In letting go. I could feel her attraction, it was strong. It was confusing; it was constantly moving away, while she was standing still.

She was saying no. She was telling me I was wrong. How dare she?

I watched her jump off the edge and begin to accelerate off into the sky.

I crouched. The chase was on! I felt my muscles bunch, ready to release.

They froze.

Later.

Wait.

I was confused. Why was I not already after her? I could easily catch her. Snatch her from the air. Take her back.

Later.

This inhibition hurt, but I couldn't work it out. I was trapped again.

I was stopping myself and didn't know why!

I screamed the frustration out of my body. I turned and blasted the bower. The fire was short lived, but was beautiful. I watched the flames consume it. They danced so prettily.

I went off to find something to fight.

Soaring out over the city I opened my heart to anger and felt it call me. There were people whose rage I could fan to a fight. Frustrations that I could nurture and bring forth as the joy of struggle.

That would make me feel better.

Maebh

As the plants closed around Bridget, I went to the task at hand. Struggling directly with the magical energy that was flowing through them. Keeping half a mystical eye on Bridget, I was able to trace it as she made her way through the mess. It was difficult; I kept switching back and forth between her and the overactive plants. Even with my focus on the plants, I was definite about when she entered the flat. That is what I assumed anyway from the magical supernova that temporarily blinded my second sight.

After the dazzling light had faded, there was a moment of shocked calm, both for me and the plants. Then all hell broke loose. The plants went from gradual invasion to complete attack mode. The after shock of the magical explosion up in the flat was still ringing in the ether. I was at the centre of the frenzy.

Switching up my approach, I was now physically ripping away at the vines that were attacking me, it was manic. The magical control wasn't enough on its own anymore. Panic gripped me, the tendrils were starting to get a hold on my ankles. The thorns were cutting my hands as I tugged at them, breaking the strands as they tried to creep higher. If it got above my knees, I would be trapped, helpless. Taking the panic, I channeled it. My heart beating faster but pumping magic as well as blood. The power began to fill me. Taking my anger and fear, I turned it outwards.

It manifested as fire.

Cocooned in flames I was safe. Barely feeling warm. The wall of fire spread out from me consuming the plants. The strands of plant that were already gripping me wilted and fell off.

"Bloody hell," I breathed, uncertain what else to say. My previous attempts to even raise enough fire to light a candle had been unsuccessfully. The effort had always just left me tired and frustrated. And still looking for matches.

The flames ended, my anger replaced by a new plateau of shock. I was standing in the centre of a charred circle, a few of the hardier bushes were still smouldering. In the silence I listened to my heart race and willed it to slow down. The immediate danger had passed, and reaching out I could tell that Bridget wasn't anywhere near by. The road back up the hill was a fairly solid wall of plants, and was the only route home.

Using the last dregs of the magical surge, I tried to heal my hands only just managing to stop the bleeding from the scratches. I was going to need them. Despite what I had said about other Witches, I doubted any would show up, there aren't that many left who fully understand. So there was no chance of the cavalry showing up. And the classic white knight tended not to come to help out Witches, call it bad press. It might have been a nice change of speed to have someone help out a bit, not because I couldn't save myself, but it was a bit tiring to have to always be your own rescuer. If there was a hero, or heroine, who might just check in on occasion to see I was alright, that would be lovely. Sighing as I knew it was pretty unlikely, I just got on with it. The price of pragmatism.

I considered the options. Looking at the charred circle again, I could try for more fire, but I didn't feel strong enough. It was impressive but I wasn't sure exactly how I did it. Experimenting would be dangerous if I couldn't control it. I was a bit scared of it, of myself. That was a lot more power than I was normally able to summon.

"Anybody got a spare machete?" I asked the universe pausing to listen. "No? Oh well." My philosophy includes the position that it never hurts to ask. It doesn't always work, but worth trying. Rolling up my sleeves I set to. I needed a path, there wasn't one so I set about making one. Using my feet, hands, and when required a bit of magical manipulation.

It was slow going. It took ages but I managed to get clear of the plants and felt done in. So I staggered across the road and set myself down on the wall to grab a wee breather. As I sat, a Council van pulled up on the other side of the road. The expressions on the faces of the workers amused me and I muttered, "Aye, good luck."

I couldn't hear what they said to each other but when they got out of the van, I decided to hide. Fading myself into the background, I waited until they were both attacking the plants with tools from the van before slipping away.

Back across the bridge I dragged myself into the nearest cafe. I needed to rest and refuel. The first coffee barely touched the sides, so I ordered another and a huge slice of the richest cake that they had.

I sipped the coffee once it arrived, now feeling able to begin replaying recent events in my mind. The overgrown plants were definitely linked to John, and Bridget had made it up to his flat. Then it was all a bit uncertain. The explosion had been powerful but hadn't felt like a battle. Just a lot of energy.

Finishing the cake and coffee, it was time to see what I could feel out in the ether. I stared into the dregs of my coffee. And opened my mind. The rush of impressions was more than I could handle so I shut my 'sight' down again. There was a distinct feeling of danger, but only a numpty would have missed that. Bridget was still out there, but not in trouble as far as I could tell. There were hints of drums and fire but it was all jumbled up. I couldn't tell if it was a memory of Beltane or something still to come.

Even that brief dip into the mystic was tiring; rubbing my eyes only helped a little. I didn't have the focus to go deeper or be more controlled. It was however reassuring that things weren't completely lost.

I paid for my coffee and cake and set out into the increasingly warm day. I needed to go home and have a bath. Freshening up would make it easier for me to use my power again. I needed to be rested to work out what was happening with Bridget. Given the heat, it would possibly need to be a cold bath. However before the bath, I had one more task. To empty my flat of all plants. Just until this had settled down, probably.

I was nearly at Princes Street when I heard Bridget in my mind. The telepathic shout taking me by surprise. It was a download of information into my brain. Normally we only used it along lines of sight, if it was important, otherwise it was literally like shouting: any sensitive person would pick up on it. Relieved that she was okay, I headed to her cottage, the bath put off until later.

At the cottage I let myself in and found Bridget at the kitchen table. We began what I felt was obviously going to be a Council of War. Bridget filled me in on what had happened, how John had been transformed and that she had interrogated him after being transported to Salisbury Crags.

I could tell that she was keeping something back, but I decided not to push her. She would have her reasons, just like I had my own reasons for leaving out the fire raising that I had achieved. It felt both too flashy and too dangerous. I wanted to think about it more before discussing it with another Witch, even my best friend.

After we had finished comparing notes Bridget outlined her plan to me. I wasn't convinced at first so we debated it. She was adamant on some points, but I was able to get her to make some changes. I felt guilty that my idea was going to make it more dangerous not less.

"So, do you think it will work?" Bridget asked me as she went to refill my wine glass. The apple wine and the fact we seemed to have a plan was restoring my calm. I shrugged nearly spilling the top-up. I was that exhausted.

"I just don't know." I nearly fumbled the glass again as I put it down. "It is an impressive idea, I'll give you that. Old magics are often the most reliable, and this is about as old school as it gets." I leant forward and cradled the wine glass in both hands. "And to be honest, I don't think that we have that many other options." The exhaustion was starting to apply a blow torch to my optimism.

"Just one final point, if this fails, you agree that we need to ask for help?" I wanted her to say it out loud. Just in case this didn't work. She will have had her three attempts and that was when it was best to admit, if not defeat, at least that more help is needed.

"Yes. I agree. If this plan fails we will be in serious trouble. All of us. Not just Witches, but the whole city, Scotland, possibly the world." Bridget nodded. I agreed with her view, from what we had seen, it had moved beyond one man's mental health being threatened by magic to a serious risk to the fabric of reality.

"Okay, then. I think I can get everything lined up for you." My mental checklist of what I would need to do already running. We didn't have much time, but we only had one shot.

"Tomorrow it is then." Bridget said with a note of finality. I could tell she wasn't happy, but we were agreed that this was the best option. She had resisted my initial suggestion, but it was important. To lure a hunter you needed to use good bait. I made my excuses and went to prepare my part of the trap.

Bridget

It was difficult to not tell Maebh the full story. But I decided that some things needed to remain private, even if they were significant. I was not under his influence any more, or more accurately I wasn't allowing my own feelings to be manifest. I was better prepared. Although I had hidden the magical gown at the bottom of a drawer. That would need to be studied later.

As hoped, Maebh had been helpful. Her suggestion on how to improve my trap made a lot of sense, even if it did make me worry about what else could go wrong. There were fewer options than I would have liked, but that was the reality of the situation. I would just have to work a bit harder to ensure that my part of the plan would be sprung before he could do any real damage to the bait. Maebh would help with that as well. You sometimes had to take big risks to get big results.

I waved Maebh off and prepared myself for a bit of old school magic. Gathering long stemmed grass from my garden and a selection of herbs and other plants which I carefully considered would strengthen the charm was just the start of it. The moss taken from the bedding was going to be at the heart of it, but there was more to this than just wishing.

After my bath I lit some incense and meditated for a while. Getting my intention into the right shape. I then set about with one of the more unusual crafting projects you will have ever seen. Pausing when necessary to shape the intent more carefully. Meditating again as required.

The spell had to be right. It had to be strong. It had to be good. The afternoon wore on slowly. I hadn't tried my hand at anything like this for a long time and my exhaustion from the morning's adventures made me slower than I would have liked.

I finally finished it just as the sun was low enough to sink below the tall buildings behind my cottage. The gentle summer gloaming settled over my home and I finally felt able to relax. Making a light supper, I focused on recovering my strength and did my best to ignore any hints of the magical activity happening out there. It was a risk to leave him unsupervised for the evening, but neither Maebh nor I was ready for a direct confrontation right now. We bided our time. Some plans take a time to evolve, and this one had some fairly important time sensitive elements. I was relieved that none of the signs of magical activity that I did pick upon were particularly strong.

Before I went to bed that night, I set a few additional wards around my cottage. I didn't think he would come for me, but I didn't want to get caught out if he did. They wouldn't keep him out for long, but they would wake me up before he got too close. It was a little bit more complex than just making sure that you had closed the kitchen window. I needed a good night's sleep, the last two days had taken it out of me and tomorrow was looking to be quite complicated as well. I settled into an uneasy sleep.

***

Opening my eyes, I saw the same panorama that I had this afternoon, but it was now night time.

A low full moon was the source of illumination.

Despite the fact it was dark, the air was warm. The air heavy with the heady scent of some invisible lilac. I was wearing the gown again. The sensation of the smooth fabric against my skin was very pleasant. I didn't remember putting it back on, had I gone sleepwalking? Had my wards failed? It should have still been hidden in the drawer.

A breeze made the fabric ripple and I shivered. Not from the cold, but as if I had been unexpectedly brushed by fingers. I began to consider the possible dangers that such a magical artefact could pose and tried to remember how I had gotten here. My thought process stopped abruptly when I heard the horn sound the first time.

It sounded again. It was not the brassy sound of a modern horn. The guttural noise was made by a real one, taken from an animal. It was exactly what I feared. With the Green Man walking free in the world, the Wild Hunt would not be far behind.

The stories crowded into my head, so many tales of death and despair. The myths drawn from multiple cultures, none of them gentle. The Elf King with his riders, Der ErlKönig, Odin's Hunt, the Hounds of Annwn. Across the world the stories came, all with a single message. Beware.

The terror that rides at night. The downfall of the unwary, the embodiment of that primal fear. What it is to be prey. Hunted.

The force that takes what it wants. Humanity has a long memory, we used to be eaten as much as we now eat. The primal brain remembers. It is hardwired into us. Fear it.

All my knowledge, the stories and myths, the science of fear and the role of amygdala. None of it matters when you hear the horn of the hunt. You know they are coming for you. My heart pounded, the blood in my veins screamed at me to run while my muscles froze. I scanned the sky looking for any hint of their approach.

There was nothing. Scanning the sky I could see a deeper darkness moving out there. Blurring the stars.

Unable to flee, I tried to calm myself. I shut my eyes, turning my thoughts inwards. To find my centre so I could protect myself with my magic. Panic kept my mind from settling. I was too tense, too fearful. A sob nearly crept from my throat. I had no choice but to wait. To pray that it would be quick.

At the last moment I opened my eyes. My curiosity was too great, I had to see what happened. There was nothing to see. I had barely realised this before I was lifted from my feet by a strong wind. Surrounded and buffeted by the energy of the hunt. I was pulled along by the invisible hunters. A human sized leaf in the arms of a gale.

As I gained height with the hunt, I saw more of the city. The strong light of the moon making clear what had happened. Edinburgh was broken.

Not entirely ruined, it was however no longer what it once had been. The ravages of nature had stripped away large chunks of the solidity of civilisation. The Parliament, Holyrood Palace and Dynamic Earth were all concealed beneath a spreading forest.

As the hunt banked over the Old Town I could see a few small glimmers of light below. The lights were warm but unsteady, the flickering of candle flames.

No electric lights pinned down the night and forced away the darkness. Night was once again ruled by darkness. The only real challengers the moon and the distant stars.

I looked closely around me and realised that the hunt was not entirely invisible. They were a shadowy mist, a deepening of the darkness of the night. Constantly changing hints of horse, hound and man appeared and disappeared around me. There was no solid form, just the idea of predators and hunters. The scent of old blood and sweat came and went. Under it all was the constant. The primal power of the hunt. It called to me. The feelings of hunger. Of speed. Of pursuit. I was terrified. I was exhilarated.

The flight path banked again coming low over the forest where the Palace used to be, beginning to descend towards the Royal Mile. The buildings here were in various states of decay, some were still standing and occupied. The telltale flickers of flame catching my eye through partially shuttered windows. As we descended lower, the darkness deepened, the buildings hid the moon, the street a black river into which the hunt plunged. Relentless in its onward flight.

As we lost the moonlight, I was briefly blind; my sight adjusted. The world became visible in a palette of grey and the mysteries of the night were revealed to me. The shadows shared their secrets. My terror began to fade. It was now just exciting. It was powerful. It felt good. Intoxicated by the effortlessness of our flight.

Rising swiftly to the height of the tops of the buildings. Rolling backwards and forwards. The Hunt was powerful but we moved without purpose. As we moved higher I saw movement below. My attention became riveted.

It was a figure. Scurrying from shadow to shadow. Making its erratic way up the hill. Huddled over and shrouded from head to foot. As if my attention had made the Hunt notice the figure, I was surrounded by sound. The Hunt gave voice. A mixture of the ancient horn, with baying and inhuman cries. I joined in. The cry ripped forth unbidden from my blood and bones. I was not with the Hunt. I was the Hunt.

The figure below was our rightful prey. It was time to chase.

Our cry startled the figure. They broke cover, just as we had hoped. The cry started the chase. The figure heading up the incline of the hill at full tilt. My hearing was sharp. I could hear the laboured breathing. It was beautiful. The most delicious taste filled my mouth. It was the tang of fear in the sweat of our prey. Our cherished one. It made my mouth water. My heart was pounding. I urged us faster and faster. The electricity flowing in my blood. I must either hunt or explode. The force too strong to contain.

I hunted.

The rolling surge of our approach filled my body. The strength in my paws, my jaws, my claws, my teeth. The muscles of all my legs bunching and releasing. My many mouths watering.

The increasing tempo bringing us closer to a wild ecstasy. As we closed with our beloved, our destiny. I was one with the whole hunt. The hunger that drove us on as one.

We closed in.

The prey, the beloved, was lost to thought now. Panic filled the air. The sweet, sweet taste of fear. As we neared, we cried out again. We would embrace our beloved and end it. The joy mounting. The cry an expression of my being. The blood called out to be spilled. I could feel the prey's heart fluttered. It was weakening.

We could tell how it would go. The destiny was clear. Our beloved prey had one final burst of energy left. The rapport between us was now unbreakable. We are one. Hunter and prey, entwined and beloved. Inseparable. The final burst of energy that drove it forward pulled us along as well. The gap shrank rather than increasing. We were in harmony. The final supernova of effort broke the prey. It stumbled. We fell.

We closed in. It was time. The final embrace. The kill. The feast.

We ripped away the cloak.

The prey looked up at us and screamed.
It was me. My face twisted in terror.
The scream came from outside and inside and tore me apart.

The world shattered.

***

I awoke in my bed, my sheets twisted and sodden with the sweat that was still dripping from my body.

Laying still in bed, it took me a few minutes to regain control of my breath. Banishing the vision of my own face twisted with terror. Quelling the thwarted blood lust that left me shaking.

I managed to slow my heart rate enough that it no longer felt as if it were trying to tunnel its way out of my chest. Fetching a glass of water, I checked all my wards. They were still intact. This was not an attack from outside.

Straightening the sheets, I took time to reflect. Why had this come to me like that? I couldn't just dismiss it. The message was clear.

My previous attempts to help John had failed as I either lacked the right insight, or I hadn't acknowledged the consequences of suppressing my own desires.

If I fell a third time, I would not be able to turn things back. The desires within me would not be tamed. I would truly become one with the Hunt.

I was both prey and predator, and I had to accept this. The plan tomorrow was going to turn that to our advantage. I just had to stay strong.

I meditated on this lesson. Settling back into bed, allowing my body to rest ahead of tomorrow's final battle.

Maebh

Bridget was ready for me when I pulled up to her cottage the next day. It was another warm day. The air was buzzing again but it was less threatening than yesterday. The mood was less desperate, more whimsical. The plants appeared to be behaving themselves, but I didn't trust the wee buggers. I was worried, not just that the plants were biding their time but about the whole plan. I did my best not to think about it. Packing the car and mild banter was about the speed of what I could handle.

"I'm surprised I've not dragged you along before to this. The Lughnasadh parties are generally really good fun. Normally we hit a beach somewhere, or a remote field. This time we're hitting Rosslyn Glen, which luckily is damn near perfect for what you need to do. As well as for the partying." I managed to fit Bridget's small pack down the side of the rest of stuff that I had been tasked with getting to the party site.

"You know me. I'm not one for crowds. And some of the hippy stuff they get up to really isn't my cup of tea. I may be a pagan but I still have some standards." Bridget sounded very haughty for the last bit of her statement. It was akin to the old Morningside stereotype. I could tell she was just poking to get me to react. The stress that we both felt about the coming day was thrumming between us. This was a good way to vent.

"Standards is it? Here I was thinking you were just a wee stuck up middle class snob. Oh well."

We both grinned, some of the tension going out of the air.

Chuckling, I squeezed the boot of the car closed. "That's that, lets hit the road." Bridget nodded and slipped into the passenger seat. We set off.

"If our plan is to work we need to get things set-up properly. Will I have time to scout around the site?" Bridget asked idly watching the streets roll past outside the car windows.

"Yes. I'm the catering lead, no surprise there, so we are part of the first wave for setting up the campsite. If you need something tweaked, I will do what I can. Not promising a 100% success rate, as this is hippy-herding, but I can generally steer them a little bit." I saw her nod in my peripheral vision.

"That is good. We are taking a big risk getting these other people involved, but you are right. It will allow us to set a much better trap. How many people do you think will be there?"

Bridget was obviously still a bit anxious, she was used to already having the answers, but that just wasn't possible right now.

"The way the vibe is going with all this energy floating around there should be a really good turnout tonight. The plants have only been going crazy in certain places, so they haven't stopped the buses running yet. The word on the grapevine is that most normal people are a bit bemused but aren't freaking out.

The plants have gone crazy but no one has been harmed. I suspect that some of them are just enjoying being unexpectedly horny to care about noticing anything strange. So that means my hippy lot, with their more open attitudes, are in their element.

So they are much more likely to show and want a really good time tonight. It is best that they don't know what it actually going on. They once debated the meaning of meaning for the better part of two hours. Interesting but not helpful in a discussion that was trying to reach an actual decision on a different topic."

The philosophical debate that followed as we drove out of town was a pleasant way to distract us from what was coming later.

***

We were the first to arrive at the secluded spot that had been picked for the party. As the afternoon wore on, more and more people filtered into the glen. The mood was upbeat. Bridget had been able to scout out the site and I could tell that she was pleased with the set up.

My set up had taken a bit longer than normal. The fire had been specially designed to play a pivotal role in the trap as well as needing to be suitable for cooking on. It was a masterwork of multi-tasking. The general ebb and flow of the energy was being fed gradually into the heart of the campfire.

As the afternoon turned into evening, people were chatting and chilling out, each one of them bringing their energy to the gathering. As the mood built from chilled to excitement and pleasure-seeking, a few of the keener people began to drum. My other duties were keeping me focused on the food, but I could feel the swell of energy as a gentle thrum underneath everything. The first wee hints of the aroma from dinner floated up. Teasing my tastebuds, promising a fine feast soon.

As I had been pottering around earlier, relieved that Roslin Glen hadn't gone as wild as parts of town I had been amused by a chat I overheard. I had to bite my lip to keep from smiling.

"Have you heard about the plants growing weirdly? I think it is an experiment." Hippy One.

"Oh, mind control or GMO?" Hippy Two.

"GMO? Oh, I'd not thought of that. It is a possibility - plants don't do that naturally. It is obviously something that has gotten out of hand. But I thought it was a chemical agent, some sort of super fertiliser." Hippy One replied.

"I heard that it was for a film," interjects Hippy Three who was just passing and hadn't been involved in the discussion up to this point.

I bustled around enjoying eavesdropping as the discussion devolved into the back and forth of the varying conspiracy theories that were the individual baby of each of the participants.

Oddly none of them seemed to think it was due to a friend of theirs channelling magical energy which was unleashing the forces of nature to suit his changing whims.

As the group grew, Bridget went off to one side, nodding to anyone who came close but very much keeping herself apart. I could tell her eyes were not focused on the scene in front of her. She tended to be very visual in her understanding of magic so she zoned out more obviously when she was working powerful magic.

She had warned me to keep a tight lid on things until the power had built to the right level. It needed to be a slow burn. The trap we were building required just the right balance of energy.

"Are we really doing this?" I projected the thought along my line of sight to her, hoping it was discrete enough that none of the other sensitive people would pick up on it.

"Yes, we have to. I didn't tell you but I dreamt last night about what it would be like if we lost this time. It wasn't good." Bridget responded in the same way, her eyes fixing onto mine.

"Oh." I thought back, uncertain what else to say. *"Okay. Tell me about it later okay?"* I suppressed my curiosity as I was certain that it would just scare me right now.

"I will. It is nearly time. You have done a good job, I can feel the power pooling here. A few more people and a bit more time and the trap will have all the bait it needs." Bridget responded.

She was right. The group was growing and the atmosphere was charging up. It was just a good party vibe. That was what we needed.

As the sun sank towards the west, our position down in the glen created a false horizon, bringing us an early gloaming. The sky was still bright, but it felt like we were in a different world. The time was getting closer. Bridget's eyes on me were like a tap on the shoulder. I turned back to see her standing, ready to leave the clearing. I nodded to her. She bobbed her head and disappeared between the trees.

"Okay folks, time to get this thing burning brighter! And also to really get the dancing started!" The main fire was piled a fair bit higher from the stack that I had ready for this very moment. I had included some more ritually significant wood to help focus the spell. The tendency towards pyromania in most of the community made it easy for this to be achieved. The fire roared.

I was fortunate that in addition to my cooking prowess, I had also led the drummers a few times and designed some 'beats' for them. This made the next step of the plan much easier to achieve, even if I did it in a more devious way than normal. The drummers had been jamming some of their pre-practiced rhythms and it sounding good, but I needed something more specific.

I clapped out a few brief sequences to give them the idea and stepped back. Using the natural connection that they felt to each other from being a well practiced group, I reached out and opened the channels a little bit wider. The telepathic link was just down at the primal level.

Synchronising their muscle movements rather than linking their conscious minds. This made it easier for me to reinforce the pattern that I needed them to play. They were skilled players one and all, so all I had to do was feed them a core rhythm.

I then let nature take over so they either copied it or automatically filled in the gaps and added more nuance.

It built the next element of the trap, it was the beacon. Music and magic combined.

The beat was designed to bypass the brain and make your feet do their thing and take your heart and soul along for the ride. The brain could come if it could keep up. It was barely a blink before the dancers came up and began to do their thing around the fire. The final part of the trap.

I was now caught in the web of my own making. Just as much part of the trap as any of them. We were the bait. It went some small way to reducing my guilt, but it was still there. It was a huge risk, but the options were limited. I just hoped that Bridget was able to do her part. If not, it would be a fight for our lives.

I allowed the energy to flow and build around and within me. We were now a beautiful magical beacon. One that would lure John to his final appointment with the Witch Doctor.

Green-John

I stood over the broken and bruised people. I was the last man standing.

The fight had been what I needed.

It had been so easy to find people whose rage was close to the surface.

I barely needed to coax the ember into the flame that reaffirmed the life within us.

The warm glow of success washed over me.
It lingered until that evening and I was still smiling when I drifted off to sleep.

It had been a glorious, if low-key, battle.
Maybe next time we would take it to the death.

The blood spilt had not been much, but had sufficed for the day.

I woke the next morning to another beautiful day.

The joy at the memory faded.
Something was dimming the sunshine.

There were no clouds, but it did not warm me like it had.

There was a need unmet.

I felt alone.

I needed company.

I spent the day wandering through crowded places, reading people's moods and minds. There was little simple joy. I tried to stir some of them to happiness, but it was not easy. Their energy was not right. I needed to find something different.

I wandered all across the city. It was as the sun was starting to sink that I came to another green space. It was in the south, beyond Morningside, a fragment of memory surfaced. The park was sheltering against a hill and so it was starting to grow darker. I thought I would rest and reconnect to the ground when I heard the laughter of a child.

So cheerful. That is what I lacked! Joy! Someone untainted by worry. He would be my play fellow. I stepped forward to the edge of the tree line. I beckoned him to join me.

"Joshua! Home time." A man I hadn't seen was calling him from further across the clearing. My prospective playmate turned without seeing me and ran towards him.

"Yes Daddy!" he shouted while running full pelt. I watched as his father scooped him up and spun him around. The laughter that flowed from him was musical.

As they turned to head off out of the park, Joshua's eyes met mine over his father's shoulder and widened. He clutched his father more tightly. I could sense his fear and wonder. I raised my hand in salute.

"What is it Joshi?" the man asked, half turning. I decided to conceal myself from him.

"The man. In the woods." Joshua half whispered.

"I don't see him. It doesn't matter, let's get you home."
His father said after casting a quick glance over the
clearing. I remained invisible to him. I began to follow
them.

"Joshua. My dear Joshi, don't be afraid. I am a friend. I
just want to play. I mean you no harm." I projected the
thought to him, trying to calm him.

"Daddy, he is following us." Joshi whispered in a tight
little voice. His father stopped and looked around.

"I really don't see anyone Joshi. Is this a game?" his father
asked, his eyes uselessly scanning over where I stood. My
concealing glamour holding firm. "There is a bit of mist,
and a bush, but I don't see a man." The man held his son
more tightly to his chest and began walking again.

"No! Not a game. Scary man." Joshua burrowed closer
into his father but glared at me over his father's shoulder.

"Joshi, calm down. Your father can neither see, nor hear
me. I am lonely and would like you to be my friend.
Would you like to come with me? There will be games,
and soon lots of friends to play with. And beautiful flowers
and trees and we can dance across the sky." I felt upset he
was rejecting me. I only wanted to share in the simple fun
he had been having. It had gotten lost somehow. I was
surprised when he projected a thought back at me. He had
a strong mind.

"No! Bad man! I don't go with strangers!" The thought was powerful and I reeled back. I was a little affronted that he thought I was dangerous. There were hints within his thoughts of a real fear, a darkness that made no sense to me. A lesson that had taken root that only badness came from strangers. I was shocked that anyone would want to threaten this innocence. How could he have learnt this danger? I despaired that people had become so cruel that a child had to defend itself. That joy was a threatened commodity.

"Now wait Joshi..." I began. I stopped. Nothing I could say would help. My very presence threatened his childish joy, his innocence the very thing that I wanted to relearn. I didn't want to end it. Magic made me strong but it didn't make me happy. I wanted to laugh, I wanted to run, I wanted to spin around until I fell over giggling. I watched them go. My heart heavy that this world contained people who could cause such fear in an innocent.

And then I felt something. A sudden blazing energy. Off to the south and East.

It was Bridget. She was calling me. There was so much power. She had changed her mind! I could tell she was not alone. She was building the hunt for me! It felt so good. The power was stirring me. I must go to her.

"Farewell Joshi. Good night." I cast the thought at him and took to the sky.

Bridget

Leaving Maebh at the fire, I wandered a short distance into the woods. I pulled along behind me an invisible strand of magic, connecting me back to the part of the trap that she was building. Once I reached the bivouac I had built, I wove the energy around myself in a living net of power. It continued to grow with strength every minute, drawing energy from the fire.

I had selected this spot as I needed to be close, but not actually in the middle of the party. It would have been difficult to stay in a trance in the middle of the party, and I would have just been in the way. And that would have prevented me from springing the trap. I was not fond of the term 'astral projection', it was overused and tended to make people think in a fixed way, but it was the closest term I was comfortable with that described sort of what I was doing.

The phrase 'Soul walking' sounded far too twee. It was also far too unwieldy to say I was putting myself into 'the state of consciousness during which I can perceive reality via the medium of the currently unnamed level of reality where the energy which permeates everything can be seen and shaped if directed by a trained consciousness such as mine.' So astral projection it was.

Opening my awareness to the world, the net of energy that I had pulled around myself came into focus. A constantly shifting arrangement of strands of pulsating energy that were fed by an unspooling ribbon of warm light from the group gathered at the fire.

On this level, the forest was brighter than the dusky 'real' version I had left behind. The life energy within all the plants and trees provided a background over which the magical forces played and flowed freely. I tapped into it and allowed it to add to my own strength. Once I had adapted to the enhanced level of power, I reached out and called to John. I could feel him respond immediately.

It was like a thread attached to my heart had suddenly been pulled tight. I could feel him getting closer. The feedback was both exciting and scary. He was even stronger than before. As he neared, the shape of the world around me changed. The free flowing energy took on new shapes and changed the appearance of the forest. Standing in a small clearing, there was bright sunshine cutting through the trees and dappling the ground. It was an echo of the glade that he had created in his flat, but mapped onto the local forest. I could still sense the fire and the hippies not very far away. He was close but I couldn't see him yet.

"You ran earlier, I almost chased you. Something held me back. Maybe it was better I waited. This is so much more rewarding. I presume you have changed your mind? Otherwise why would you be calling me?" The tone of voice was dripping with satisfaction. I was slightly relieved. He was easier to handle when he was in a good mood. I scanned the woods, still unable to make out any sign of him. He was both a skilled hunter and this was a mystical projection, so he would be able to hide in lots of different ways. I was relieved when he stepped out of the shadow of a tree just a few feet away from me.

Having regained my bearings in the new setting, I worked out how far the heart of the trap was. It was going to be a close run thing. The muted echoes of the drums gave me both direction and hope. He may have slightly rewritten the appearance of the environment but we were still on the footing that I needed us to be on for my plan.

"I had to get away from you, the temptation that you offer was nearly too much for me to resist. I pick my battles when I can. I wanted to see you again. That is why I called you." I hoped that the entirely honest words I was using would disguise my real intent. I slipped my hand into my pocket to check that the vital part of my plan was still with me in this version of the projection. It was still there, or at least the equivalent symbol of it on this plane.

"Battles?" the John figure asked, tilting his head inquiringly "But we should not be at war! We are good together. We would be powerful. We would be happy. I can feel the people over there by the fire, you are connected to them. You called them here. It is like an offering. Would you be my priestess? Shall I be your god?

The power of the dance grows. The blood is stirring. They are opening themselves to the world, to my power. Soon they will be able to lose themselves in the energy. I will be there, waiting. Offering them my hand. They will come to me willingly. I will have my companions. We will ride as the hunt, once the need rises in us."

The John-shaped figure strode around the clearing, I kept on turning to face him. Watching enthralled as he tried to persuade me, not realising that his plan was confirming my worst fears. I concealed any signs that might give me away.

"You would be with us. I can sense within you that you have this drive, that you deny it. The passion that you bottle up. You would be strong in the hunt. You would bring so much. Give yourself the freedom to say yes! Let go of this half-life. It would be sweeter if you came to me before the others. Join me and embrace your instincts." He held out his hand to me. Offering me power, and passion. All I would have to do is give myself. I took half a step towards him, watching the joy brighten in his eyes.

The courtly gesture seemed simple, but I knew that once I gave in, it would not be elegant. It would be fire, blood and death. It was attractive and terrifying. I steeled myself again.

"It must be a battle! This is not something I pick lightly. You are undoing the balance both in the world and definitely within the poor man you claim you still are." Now was the time to act. I knew I would give in if he pushed me. Doing the right thing was not easy.

"I think I've worked it out. How you are both a man and a god, but somehow neither completely at the same time." He was puzzled by my refusal, through our connection I knew he could feel my yearning to give in. I ironically used the power swirling around us to keep myself firm in my resolve. His eyes went flat, but unreadable rather than dangerous.

"Go on," he urged seemingly willing to humour me.

"You are John, but not his conscious self. You are the passions of a normal man, merged and supercharged with the spiritual power that underpins the natural cycle.

The connection to the magical world that John could not consciously accept, due to his over-rationality, merged with his primal desires and became more than he could repress. It made you. Both more and less than a man."

He smiled at me with just his mouth, the flat eyes made it felt like he was mocking me. The situation needed to be more scientific so I added.

"To put this into psychoanalytical terms for you if you will pardon the pseudo-Freudian approach. Your Ego has been suppressed somehow in this mess and the supercharged Id has been re-integrated into this body by your Super Ego. It has combined the power with the ideas of the Green Man that lingered in your memory. Does that sound better?"

I watched him closely, praying that I was correct. Hoping that for some reason logic would weaken the hold it had on him. If I were wrong, if my magic failed us, we were all doomed to live under the rule of this mad demi-god. One who, thanks to me, would be supported by the wild hunt.

"I would say that it was interesting but I'm afraid it's not. As frankly I'm not interested." He shrugged and began to pace around the clearing, stalking me again.

"I am the force and the passion. I care not that you think you have it solved. False restraint is a denial of life. I seek to bring all life to full fruit. Your words are just that, empty words. You deny the life that pumps through us all."

I was watching him closely and had the barest moment of warning that I was in danger. His eyes came alive and bright with hunger.

I dropped to the ground and rolled, feeling the ivy tendrils shoot past where I had just been standing. I could see them in my peripheral vision snaking around trying to entwine themselves around me. I used my momentum to get to my feet again and start running.

I could hear John chuckling behind me. It was a scary-sounding joy. It was an echo of the blood lust I had felt in the hunt, made into a laugh. My perception slowed. The reality of the threat to me was real, this may be the astral plane but I could very easily die here. Possibly even easier here than in the physical world, since even a wrong thought could be fatal.

I headed out of the clearing which had been made by Green-John's thoughts, racing towards the spot where the fire blazed its way into this plane. The trap was now sprung. If I wasn't quick, I wouldn't survive the confrontation.

"Time to find out if I'm right." I panted as I ran through the trees. The distance here was much greater than it had been before, I blame the distorting influence of Green-John.

I pulled tight on the ribbon of power that anchored me to the fire and the dancing hippies. The heart of the trap. I shaped a new path. I could feel John behind me, the sense that stems from millenia of mammalian survival instincts rather than anything mystical. The Hunt was on.

John

It took me a while to stop crying. It had helped a little but I now felt angry at myself. The pain I hadn't even realised had become a secret part of myself was now impossible to ignore. I jumped back into the pool. The need for action driving me to attack the mud. I threw armful after armful of it over my shoulders. Not caring where it was going or if it was helping. It just felt good to be doing something.

A few small things appeared. Other artefacts from my past. Tiny reminders of other mistakes I had made. As I saw them, I remembered the people I had neglected. None of them acted as weirdly as the frisbee or laptop, but each of them brought back a memory. All pretty bad. All part of the same damning catalogue. Looking at them, it was just the thoughtlessness of a normal man. I'm not the worst person alive, but seeing it all stacked up like that made me feel pretty shitty. I cast them aside and let them pile up on the side of the water.

After a few minutes of mud slinging, I wore myself out. The mud was still there, slightly less of it, but still enough to hide the wall. I needed another break. I was muddy and tired, so rinsing myself off I climbed back out of the water to rest on the bank. I could feel Bridget again, but there was still no sign off her. I was alone, other than my little hecklers.

I watched them picking over the items that I had thrown aside. They were looking much worse than before. The halo was gone, the horns were gone. The pitchfork and harp were nowhere to be seen.

Now they had lost these add-ons, I found they looked more familiar than they had before. I couldn't put my finger on it, but they looked like they were part of something else I knew. From a different context.

They weren't even heckling each other anymore. The lack of banter was making me uncomfortable. I flopped down and stared into the water.

"I wonder what Bridget is doing?" It was more to break the silence, but I was genuinely curious. I missed her, although I didn't know how long she had been gone, it can't have been that long. The fact I could feel her presence but not see her was making me worried. As I watched the pool it started to darken like the frisbee had. Most of the water went flat and smooth as black glass while the outer edge began to swirl around it. The centre began to brighten, misty shapes and blurred movements let me see that something was coming. I settled down to see what was going to happen next.

As the image came into focus I could see Bridget in a forest glade talking to me. There was something about it that all looked just a bit wrong.

"I don't remember this. I've never been in a forest with Bridget." I was very confused.

"This isn't a memory, this is now." the angel informed me. "This is what is happening outside of your mind." It sounded oddly flat. I had imagined a depressed angel.

"Yeah, out where the real fun is!" the devil added. Sounding a bit happier than the angel but was still sounding whiny.

"This is what I want! You stay here, forget about all that stuff and just enjoy the ride." He was eagerly watching the water but was waving me away.

"How long have I been here? It only feels like a couple of hours. Is it longer?" I saw the pair of them exchange a quick glance and avoid looking at me. It was worrying that neither of them seemed willing to answer.

"I want to see what this means! You can show me. Do it now!" I ordered glaring at them. All they had done was hint towards things and irritate me. I wanted some answers. They did what I told them but with much dragging of feet and awkward shuffling.

They took up position. One on either side of the pool and each dipped a hand into the water. The water by the devil's hand began flowing as a band of red, swirling and glowing. Similarly white light sprang from the angel's hand and formed the inner band of colour. The central disk now framed by their mystical contributions.

"You want to know what it means? This is what will happen if you do not end the imbalance that brought you here." They spoke together but slightly out of tune with each other. It just sounded really creepy. It was possibly made worse by the fact they were finally in agreement. "This is what will follow if things continue as they are now."

The vision of Bridget and myself in the wood disappeared from the central disc.

It changed and started showing a range of different images. It had to be the future they warned me of.

I saw the destruction of Edinburgh. I saw myself leading an army that flew in the night and took people for our entertainment. Buildings destroyed as trees and plants grew wildly. Roads and trains disappeared under new forests. Miles of dead street-lights where the power had failed and darkness now returned. Bridget was at my side, but any hint of the kindness I had seen in her was now gone. She was a warrior-witch who fought alongside me. Using her power to harm and kill at my command. There was joy. I could see the joy, but it was all from selfish pleasure or from hurting people. I was to become a king over a new dark age.

"I don't want that!" I shouted at them. Hoping that just by saying no I would be able to prevent it happening. The power was exciting, but the price was far too high.

"Stop. I don't want to see any more. Come here." I ordered them. They removed their hands from the water and the coloured streams disappeared. As they did so the image wavered and returned to the scene of Bridget. She was now running through the woods, dodging through the trees. From her face she looked determined rather than frightened.

I looked at my hecklers as they sat quietly waiting for what I do next. The final piece of the puzzle clicked into place.

"I've worked out what you remind me of now. I can see you more clearly, but you are still in disguise. I think I was blind not to see it before.

The colours should have given it away! I think I need to help you."

I reached down and placed a hand on each of them. I thought more clearly about what they meant to me and what I had been hiding from myself.

They shimmered and changed. The wings and goat legs vanished. Either side of me, instead of a devil and an angel were a 'Red' and a 'White'. The companions to the May Queen and Green Man from Beltane. The representatives of change and stability. The irresistible force and the immovable object. The duality of nature that I had ignored. The fact I was more than one thing.

"That's better." I said and we settled down to watch things unfold in the pool.

Bridget

The mood of the forest had changed, the sunshine had gone. The previous warm early afternoon vibe was now a brooding dusk. The influence of John's hunger for the chase and my fear fueling the change. Seeing the world in this dark mirror of my feelings only strengthened my growing terror.

I could now see the fire ahead of me, just beyond the next few trees, but despite the short distance in the real world it eluded me. Its mirage-like qualities made it feel close but unobtainable. I could feel the pull of it and the dragging fear of being pursued holding me taut between these opposing forces. I bent my will to reshape this world to bring me closer to the fire.

As I threw my energy into the struggle, every sound became magnified. My ragged breathing, the beating of my heart, every single twig snap and the rustling of the undergrowth. There is an old cliche 'do or die' but I feared that there could be worse things than dying. Death would be preferable if the alternative was trusting my fate to the probably non-existent mercy of an enraged demi-god whom I had betrayed. Pushing the sound of the hunter closing behind me from my mind, I threw all my will into the connection and pulled. It snapped into place and I was on the edge of the clearing.

The beautiful dancing shadows left a trail of sparks in the air and that fountained up from where their feet touched the ground. Flames of all colours cascaded from the circle of figures, merging with the ghost fire of the bonfire which they danced around, making an ever-changing edifice of living light.

This was the heart of the plan. Tonight was Lughnasadh. A quarter day of the Celtic calendar, a turning point of the year. It was a night of fire in the darkness. A night for remembrance of the dead with the strivings of the living. A time to celebrate the harvest, the fruit of our labours.

In the past, on this night, games had been played. Tonight the only game I was playing had the simple name 'stay alive'. Unlike the modern version of the games, this was being played for the highest stakes possible and was going to test my skills and willpower to the utmost.

Maebh and I had agreed that using the symbolism of the night, in addition to the living bait, would provide the best way to increase our chances of success. The night as a pivot point in the year was perfect to help us try and swing a change. The festival was a celebration but one that evoked competition and acknowledged death and endings. Over this, we layered the power that could be raised with fire and drums and dancing.

The people around the fire giving themselves to the natural flow of the world. The resonance growing and building. It was now the time. Deep within the flow I shaped my intent.

The energy I had spun around myself as a net I now channeled back into the fire. I augmented it and shaped it with my own will. The fire transformed into a magical maelstrom designed to destroy the magical bonds of whatever it touched.

I pulled the most important part of the plan from my pocket. It was the 'poppet' I had made of John/the Green Man. It was a simple 'corn dolly' made from grass and twigs I had gathered from my garden with, at its heart, the moss from the bed in the bower. It also contained John's hair. It was one of the oldest magics based on the principle of 'as above, so below'.

The concept of sympathetic magic that said it was possible to use the bond that existed between a person and things like their hair. I resented that more people knew about Haitian voodoo than they did about the homegrown equivalent. My plan was simple. I was not trying to hurt John which is why I moved the battlefield to the astral plane. Here I hoped that the shape of my intent would be clearer so that the fire would take the poppet and destroy the connection between John and the Green Man. And not have any physical impacts. It would allow the natural balance between the spiritual and the physical worlds to be re-established. On this plane, I hoped that the risk of his body being harmed was reduced.

Just as speech can move people, and a dream can change the world, I knew that thought has power and when used at the right time in the right place I would be able to make things happen. In the waking dream of the astral plane I was very powerful, but so was the Green Man. I hoped that this symbolic death would remain just that. If it worked, it would free the man from the magical bonds which had so distorted him and made him so dangerous to those around him.

I watched the doll in the fire. It had transformed so it looked like a miniature version of the target.

It was twisting and writhing in pain, as if it were in fact alive. I heard a scream from behind me and Green-John appeared in the glade. The shadowy dancing figures still flickered between us, and ongoing circle. He was a running human shaped torch. The spell was working. It had hit the target.

Green-John rushed towards me and I was unable to stop him as the burning hands grabbed me. I could feel the heat of his flesh, but the fire that consumed him was cold. So cold, it burnt into me. The cold fire of death.

I struggled with him. Using both the magic I had shaped and in my spirit body. I pulled and tugged trying to separate the intertwined forces that were there in front of me. I had to separate them so one could become a normal man again and the other could return to free flowing energy. This twisted version had to stop.

The burning man pulled at me screaming in his rage and pain. Struggling to continue to exist. It seemed that buried impulses and desires having found a conduit within a living entity, did not want to relinquish this new freer existence. I gritted my teeth against the pain, kept silent and continued to struggle against him.

As I grappled with him I could feel his form shift under my hands. The flesh switched backwards and forwards between human and plant. Muscles and skin becoming vines and thorns and back again. It was working, the two elements were separating. I ignored the pain in my body where his attack had burnt me. I focused on unravelling the energy but it was fighting me every step of the way.

With a final burst of desperate strength the burning figure toppled us both into the fire.

I screamed.

The full force of the magical fire now surrounded us.
I reminded me of when I had come too close to liquid nitrogen when I was a student. Someone in the lab had been fooling around and it had been much too close for comfort. I struggled harder with my patient and assailant. I was winning. He began to unravel completely in my hands, the poppet was long gone. Now the representation of Green-John on the astral plane was also gone. Both were now smoke, ash and memories. The old magic had worked.

With the struggle over, I had a split second of relief that I had won. Despite the pain, it was still a victory. This was swiftly replaced by terror as I realised that I couldn't see any way out of the fire. I had been pulled into my own trap, shaped to destroy magical bonds and it would not end well for me. Even if it couldn't destroy my body it could destroy my mind.

I pushed back against the flames and tried to sense my way out. It was difficult. I pushed myself deeper into a calm place. I could detect a thin strand of connection. I clung to it and tried to force my way along the path. Not caring where it would lead me. My arms stretched out, feeling for any respite from the freezing flames. I was blind, but optimistic.

John

I watched what had turned out to be a battle unfold. It was very weird. Bridget was clearly doing something magical. I tried not to freak out when the figure that looked like me burst into flames. I could feel it, but only as a slight tingle. The glass overhead began glowing with the same light. When they tumbled into the fire together, it seemed to ring the vision in the same way the red and white had done. It was really eerie.

As I watched, the other version of me fell to bits and disappeared; I felt a headache starting. A niggle just behind the eyes. I was also feeling lighter, a knot somewhere had loosened.

Watching Bridget, I could tell she was lost. I could feel her growing panic. I called her name, hoping she could hear me. She didn't respond to me but she looked like she was getting closer. I could now feel that she was in pain and needed help. I got on my knees and braced myself to pull. I plunged my hand into the pool to take her hand.

As soon as I put my hand below the surface, I felt her hand grip mine and she exploded out of the water as if she had been falling from a great height. I tried to control her momentum and we ended up tangled together.

I settled us by the water's edge. She sat there for a few moments breathing deeply. Bridget quickly dried in the heat of the green house. After she settled down, I could see she was looking at me very suspiciously. I was just so pleased to see her I nearly laughed.

"Hello Bridget, welcome back. You looked like you needed a hand. I saw some of what happened. That was all a bit weird, huh? It was so freaky seeing that other version of me burn up! Who was that? How was that possible? I saw a lot of it in there."

It was good to see her again and ask her to explain some more of the odd things I had seen. I waved my hand towards the water, which had returned to normal but definitely draining a lot more than it did. The hints of fire had disappeared from the glass overhead as well. It was 'normal' for what it was.

"Oh, this is back. You saw that? You saw the struggle?" Bridget went from confused to curious very quickly. "Other version? Yes, ah yes, that makes sense. It would have been freaky, yes." She was observing me closely and seemed to relax a bit more as she got to the end of the sentence.

"No. You are the one who is back. I've been here working on the problems we found when we first got here. I wondered why you had disappeared but decided I had to just get on with it. It hasn't been fun, but I decided that I should just keep at it."

I sat down next to her, making myself comfortable.

"It wasn't easy. There was a lot of rubbish blocking the channel of the stream, and I had some unhelpful helpers. Although to be fair they did help me by making the pool show what you were up to, at least the recent bit.

Oh yeah and the bigger problem if we didn't fix it. I am starting to think that it might have been longer than the couple of hours I thought it was?

It is starting to make a bit more sense to me now. God, I was a bit messed up. They helped a little."

I waved vaguely at the suddenly bashful Red and White who when they noticed Bridget looking at them faded from view.

"You were here all along? Hmm, that fits with what I suspected. Good to know. So how has it been? What have you been up to?" she asked cautiously. I could tell she was assessing me again.

"As I said, not been a lot of fun but I think it helped. I spent a lot of time digging through the mud. I thought that is what I needed to do, and maybe it was. But seeing what I've seen I think I might have been going about this the wrong way. Or at least there might be a better way. The clunky way and the symbols have been helpful, but it might be simpler.

Getting wound up by a couple of childhood stereotypes gave me the push I needed to get started. It wasn't comfortable but I needed to see how stuck I was. Raking over my past can help me see my mistakes, but I need to do more than see the past. I need to change my attitude as well. Knowledge without action is just theory. I see that now.

This whole place is wrong. It is made up of the rules that I had allowed myself to put in place, even if they were based on mistakes. This place is a symbol of the limitations that I thought I had to put on myself. Nature can't be contained like this. It isn't right! It's time for a change!"

I stood up and closed my eyes. I had said the words that came to me and it felt right. This was not how it should be. I now had an idea for how it could be different. I felt Bridget watching me. This flash of self-awareness was a more powerful feeling than when I had realised we were in my memories. I actually felt fully in control. I did what everyone has to do on occasion. I changed my mind.

Opening my eyes, I saw the bricks and high glass dome that encased the garden waver and disappear. In front of us, the pool disappeared as the streams realigned themselves. They could flow freely now that the wall was gone. The feeling of the garden changed subtly and became more like a meadow. A low fence appeared marking out the cultivated section from the wider horizons that now appeared visible beneath a glorious blue summer sky.

"Here we go, much more natural. But not without limits." I offered Bridget my hand to help her stand.

"I like what you've done with the place." She commented and then started laughing. "Don't mind me. Just not the first time I've said that recently."

I decided not to ask. We started walking back towards the incongruous archway. I noted the trestle for the vines had gone as part of the rearrangement. Bridget was still holding something back. I was more in control of myself so I knew better what I had to do.

"Don't worry Bridget. I seem to understand things better at the moment. I must have seemed so stupid to you before. I don't know how long it will last, so I want to say thank you. In case I don't remember afterwards.

I saw what you did, and seeing the glimpse of the future scared me a lot. So I can guess a bit of what was happening as well, and that can't have been fun. I think you needed to break the link for me, and I think I needed to work out the mess that made this possible in the first place. I can't change the past but I am no longer hiding from myself and that will help. So what happened to each of us was necessary for different reasons.

I hope that this makes sense. I hope I remember some of this. God, the world is a lot weirder than I thought. I want to make better choices. I think that much at least will stay with me. It already feels like it is fading. Thank you again." I felt like I was rambling but I had to say what I could. As I said my final thank you, the world faded to white.

Bridget

The shock of a hand grabbing mine was intense and quickly followed by relief. I was free of the trap. I felt myself pulled upwards and the return of warmth felt painful but fantastic. I looked around in confusion. I was back in John's greenhouse illusion. He was standing there, smiling at me. Was it a trick? Had he escaped the trap and taken us down to a different level? Looking closely, I realised that this was definitely John. The entirely human version.

My exhaustion and my curiosity were in conflict. I had so many questions, but I was mentally shattered. The last conflict in the fire had taken a lot out of me. I suppressed the vague feeling of hysteria when I accidentally echoed the conversation I had had with the other version of John in the outside world. It was definitely too much. I listened to John's explanations and felt vindicated that it meshed so neatly with what I had eventually worked out from the external clues.

As he explained his version of events, I felt my grip on consciousness weakening. It all rapidly began to turn white. I tried to tell him that he was welcome as he thanked me again. After the white, it went black and I jolted back into my body. I felt hands on my shoulder shaking me and Maebh's voice calling me.

"Bridget? Wake up! Talk to me! Are you okay?" She sounded really quite concerned so I pulled myself out of the comfort of my numbness to respond. I gasped from the pain and the sudden shock of cold and damp as she put a compress on my face.

"Ouch. Yes. I'm awake. I'm back. I think it worked. What did you see? How bad is it?" I did my best to reassure her and get her assessment of what had happened since we parted to set the trap.

"It looks like you got a bad case of sunburn, but I am guessing it is more than that since it isn't dawn yet. I think we won. It certainly feels like the energy has gone back to normal." Maebh seemed to be more focused on me than on telling me what had happened.

"I'm fine. Tell me what happened from your side of things? Is everyone okay?" I was insistent, but decided to remain lying down while I let Maebh update me. The reality that even the purely psychosomatic side-effects of magic were painful was draining. The exertions of the magical working had left me with very little reserve and I had to keep myself together to ensure it was truly over.

"Okay." Maebh sounded doubtful, but I kept staring at her until she carried on. "After you left, things went pretty much how we planned. The forces built up exactly like we had hoped. I could feel you channelling it off, but the flow was strong at that point.

It got a bit intense. I am guessing about the time that you made contact with John. It took all my strength not to become completely submerged into the power. The rhythm was as hypnotic as we thought.

I think a few of the dancers are going to be blistered, they kept it up for quite some time. It was a good few hours of dancing. Not long after the pull had nearly got me, I became aware of the plants waking up.

I was lucky that they were all pulling towards the power, rather than attacking us. If they had gone for us, I think we would all be goners now."

I nodded, the side-effects made sense. The fact that my few minutes of interaction on the astral plane had been hours on this level made sense. The theory of relativity will need to be updated when they get able to measure and understand that level of reality. The presence of the conduit of the energy was going to make things a bit more heated.

"That sounds about right. Did you pick up any hints of what I was doing?" I asked, trying to get the whole story.

"Not really. Once the trap was triggered I could tell something had changed. The plants seemed more scared than before and the dancers began to get more frenzied. The first clue I had that something had finalised was when John materialised amongst the dancers and collapsed.

That broke the focus. They thought he was a dancer who had taken a tumble. I think I was the only one who saw that he had materialised out of the fire. He was only slightly scorched, similar to you, but he was a bit more sun-tanned already. You really don't get out enough you know."

Maebh shut up quickly when I glared at her as she transitioned from the relevant update into passing comment on my complexion and habits.

"And so I helped them drag John into one of the tents and left someone who is first-aid trained looking after him. He was completely spark out, but that doesn't surprise me. He was still breathing though."

I nodded, absorbing this update. It all sounded about right.

"Go on." I urged her, reaching for the bottle of water I could see down by her knee. I took a careful sip and the cooling sensation of the water spread all the way down to my stomach. While the fire had been cold, my skin, even on the inside, felt as if it were recovering from a bad burn.

"I'd only just made it back out of the tent when I saw you appear out of the fire as well. It was lucky everyone was being busy, nosing around at the other dramas; that was a fairly dramatic entrance. How did you get there? Why did you end up moving?" Maebh asked, now as curious as I had been to hear the other side of the story.

"It was as bad as we feared. The bait was exactly what he wanted. He was so strong. I nearly didn't make it to the fire after he appeared and the poppet worked. Possibly too well. He came at me a blazing human torch. I didn't have time to avoid him and we ended up wrestling inside the astral fire.

After the spell had destroyed his avatar, I was left alone. I was trapped. I was looking for any way out, and found a faint psychic thread. It brought me back to the construct that John had shown me in his trance. I found the old part of John there, he said he had been stuck there the whole time.

He was setting things to rights from the inside as well apparently." I sipped some more water, enjoying the returning feeling of life.

"That explains why you look like you've been tanned, but why did that move you?" Maebh asked, wringing out and re-dampening the cloth on my face. It felt good.

"I'm not sure. The astral plane distorted when Green-John arrived and maybe being pulled into the fire might have dragged more of my essence into the astral plane.

It is more dangerous than I'd ever try. Transforming yourself entirely into displaced energy is a risk and power beyond me. I think that there was too much magic sloshing around and it bent the world further than we thought. I'm just glad that it was only astral fire.

It hurts a lot, but it could be worse. I will heal. This is not going to be easy but I'm going to need your help. I need to see him on this plane. The construct was convincing but I don't trust it entirely. It was the power spilling out into the physical world that was the problem." Maebh tried to dissuade me but I struggled up and refused to let her win this argument.

"Are you sure? I saw him, he seemed normal. Unconscious but normal." Maebh tried to encourage me to rest one final time with gentle pressure on my arm. I winced.

"Ouch. Sorry, but yes. It isn't that I don't trust you. I don't trust the energy to just give up. I broke the link so I know it isn't still flowing, but I need to know that he isn't holding any in reserve. He was fairly controlled in the psychological construct, I need to know this wasn't a fake out." I made it to my feet and out of the tent, grateful that Maebh tended to have the more palatial end of the canvas equipment at her disposal.

"Okay. I obviously can't stop you." Maebh's tone made it clear that she wished she could.

"You are going to need to do more than not stop me. Help me! Which tent is he in?"

I looked around the dim campsite. The fire was still burning but now much lower, people huddled in cloaks watched the dancing flames closely. I envied them their relaxed mood and suppressed the pang of guilt that I had probably driven them to exhaustion. I had my share of that, so shifted more of my weight onto Maebh's arm.

"This way." Maebh edged us towards one of the nearby tents. I stumbled a little on an invisible guy-rope, the banality of the incident helped me feel more grounded. This was definitely real, I just needed to make the final test of my patient.

Maebh went a little ahead and did her best to scatter the ministering 'sprites' since angels felt out of place in this setting. She handed me her head torch before I went in and then stood guard outside while I hunkered down next to John to make my final assessment.

On visual inspection, he seemed to be back to normal. The skin tone had gone back to what I remembered from Friday night, and the natural softness had returned to his face. He looked quite sweet.

Next test. I rested my hand on his forehead, to get the skin-to-skin connection. I was relieved that instead of a discharge of magic, all I felt was the warm, possibly slightly feverish skin, of a human. It was so slight that I had no fear that he was in any medical danger. It was just a natural side effect of what we had gone through. He was going to be fine on that basis.

I decided I need one final check. I gently touched his shoulders and rocked him a little.

"John! Wake up!" I urged him, calm but authoritative. My magical senses gave no flicker of anything. He began to stir from the increased contact and movement. I was not going to let him stay under. I needed to see his eyes. I think he muttered my name. His eyelids flickered open and the pupils contracted in the bright light of the head-torch, obviously dazzling him. His eyes had changed back, the supernatural brown had receded back to his normal blue. There was not a glimmer of magic in them. The windows of the soul showed that he was back in charge of his own body.

"Bridget." He croaked. He would obviously need some water too, so I handed him the remains of the bottle I had started.

"Here you go. The good news is you are cured. The bad news, you are going to ache for a few days."

I let him settle back. Sensing his relief at the rehydration and my reassurance.

"Oh. Thanks." He managed to murmur before he was reclaimed by exhaustion. The bottle forgotten as his body overruled him and opted for a healing sleep. I didn't blame him one bit. I made my way back out of the tent.

"It is all good. We are done. He is cured." I silently thanked the universe that we were done.

"Thank the gods for that!" Maebh responded and pulled me into a hug. I winced but gently returned it.

"Can you take me home? I'm going to need to get some sleep in a proper bed before work," I asked Maebh, allowing her to guide me back towards the tent. It was going to be a long day, but the work was well done.

The sky was not yet lightening, but I knew it was going to be a beautiful day.

45388913R00153

Printed in Poland
by Amazon Fulfillment
Poland Sp. z o.o., Wrocław